Ellie Iulio 2013

GW00390870

# THE LUCKIEST MAN IN THE WORLD

## MIM SCALA

This novel is loosely based on the true story

of

Emilo Scala the man who won £335,000 on the Irish Sweepstake in 1931. Some names have been changed and some characters have been invented.

Copyright © 2012

ISBN-13 978-1481006255

ISBN-10: 1481006258

Emilio Scala lifted the heavy iron kettle from the stove that heated the cottage, a one-up one-down brick and granite building put up when the railway was built, specifically to house the bachelor porters that carried early travellers' luggage. Nowadays passengers carried their own. He poured boiling water into the enamel bowl and set about scrubbing his hands, taking extra care with his fingernails. His customers would look at his well-kept hands and feel confident that the ice cream he sold them was not only delicious, but pure and made with care.

Emilio heard the kids in the yard and the steady swish of his wife, Nazarene's, broom pushing dust over the cobblestones. A shard of broken mirror shaped like an abstract Mount Igor leaned precariously against the plaster wall, balancing on the heads of two rusty nails. He examined his handsome craggy face; he had inherited the blue eyes from the Milanese branch of his family. He combed the waves of black hair back from his prominent forehead, ignoring the growth of beard; DeMarco could shave him later. Yeah, a clean white shirt, there was always a clean shirt; she was a good wife. He pulled on his trousers fastened the brass buckle of his belt. Nearly ready.

He drained the thick black coffee from the mug, leaving a line of grouts on the white china, and laced up his shoes. Taking his jacket from the hook behind the door, he walked from the kitchen, into the yard.

His three kids played at polishing his ice cream tricycle. Even if he said so himself, it was the prettiest ice cream bike in south London: a copper rim on the stainless-steel lid, shining spokes in the wheels, and the paint job, done for him by Cellini as a break from the Fun

Fairs and circuses he usually decorated.

Removing the lid Emilio, started to fill the shining tub with huge ladles full of fresh glistening vanilla ice cream. Nazarena had made just the right amount in the old hand-cranked mixer. White frozen air streamed up like smoke from the packing of card ice that was used as a freezing agent. His wife watched as Emilio transferred the card ice from the mixer and packed it around the tub in the tricycle.

"Gumbah! You better get moving I can hear the train coming."

Emilio looked up at her; she looked nice, her spotless white apron wound tightly around her ample body.

"Si, si I'm one my way."

Little Joe Emilio's eldest child gave a last polish to the handlebars with his little duster. Emilio put on his jacket and climbed into the saddle. With a wave, he pedalled over the cobbles, the bouncing tricycle chased by the kids. They stopped at the yard gate and waved their father off. The ground shook as the train rumbled on the viaduct overhead. Emilio cycled into the station just as the nine o'clock Clapham train clanked to a standstill on the bridge. A loud throaty toot sent clouds of white steam and smoke cascading over the bridge and onto the road below. The smoke cleared. There he was, Scippio, a good worker; not yet fifteen and orphaned, he lived with Mrs. Manzi, who did laundry for those who could pay for it.

"Scippio you wanna work today?"

The good-looking lad ran over to the tricycle, his curls bouncing on his forehead.

"Si, Signor Scala. I always wanna work."

Scippio pulled off his cap; more dark curls bounced out of it. He

3

waited for Emilio to climb off the bike.

"Good, show me your hands."

Scippio held out his hands for Emilio's inspection, turning them this way and that and over and over like he was doing a magic trick.

"That's good, you keep them like that. Now, take the ice cream to the park, and when you sell out you come and find me. I going to play cards at DeMarco's".

"Si, Signor Scala, I sell out real quick, and I bring you the money."

"Eh. Scippio! You no say where I am." Emilio winked at the boy as he climbed proudly into the saddle of what he considered to be the most beautiful ice cream tricycle in the world, and with a pat on the back from his benefactor, rode off whistling through his perfect young teeth towards his customers in Battersea Park. Emilio took off his bicycle clips, produced a half-smoked cheroot from his jacket pocket, lit it by thumb-nailing a match, and strode off past the white tiled walls of the soda water factory into one of the labyrinth of narrow Battersea streets.

Some of the housewives were already sweeping their doorsteps and chatting to each other. Emilio felt lucky today. He had decided almost as he woke up this morning that today was a day to play cards. Passing a row of two-storey houses, Emilio stopped to bang on the window of a slightly shabby one.

"Eh. Bellucci, get up, come and play some cards."

The window slid up, and a fat head poked a sleepy, unshaven face through the clean but faded net curtains.

"What time you call this?"

"Time to play cards, come on catch me up."

Emilio strode off; as he walked, he noticed that even in this stinking depression, some of these little houses still managed to look neat and tidy. Bright doors of varying colours ranged like bunting all the way down the street. At the next corner, a fat, puffing Bellucci caught him up. Emilio punched him on the arm.

"What kept you?"

"I've been playing cards all night; I went potless about four o'clock. I came home to get some sleep."

"Who's winning?"

Bellucci screwed up his face.

"DeMarco, he's got the luck of the devil."

At the end of the street, a red and white pole stuck out of the first-floor window like a stunted medieval lance. A small swinging sign read DeMarco, Barber. The door had a blind pulled down and a 'closed' sign. Emilio opened it; followed by Bellucci, he walked down the three steps into the smoke-filled room. A single light bulb hung in a green shade over the card table. The place smelt of eau de cologne and cheap cigar smoke. There they were, the gamblers. Not big time Monte Carlo-type gamblers, but addicted nevertheless. Guys who would on a good hand risk a week's wages and the wrath of their wives.

Alonzi, a waiter at the Dorchester, sat in shirtsleeves; a stainless-steel gas-fired towel steamer bubbled away in the corner behind him. The steam from it gave the impression that it came from his prominent ears, which appeared to be fixed like large shells to the side of his peanut-shaped head.

Gambini, a bad poker player, his head framed by the Primo Carnera poster on the wall behind him, fiddled with his moustache; the boys loved him. Next to him sat Corsini, a man with the big hands and veined forearms of the stonemason that he was. He made beautiful gravestones for the local undertaker, specialising in marble angels, but these days found himself chiselling names and dates on granite slabs.

Next was DeMarco, the Barber himself—a preposterous figure, really, potbellied with a tight waistcoat and suit, a fat moustache hanging beneath the big nose on his greasy face, and woman's hands, dainty little things. He sat with his two barber chairs behind him like impoverished thrones.

Then there was Duccio, a small, tight, vain little man, who wore a permanent hat to cover his bald head. Emilio had never seen him without it. The gamblers sat around a table in the centre of the room, a shaded light bulb hanging from a brown braided flex above them. Emilio took the last chair from its place against the wall and pushed it into the table between Duccio and Alonzi.

"Buona sera, amici. I feel lucky today—deal me in."

He placed two half crowns on the table in front of him.

"Eh, Rothschild, I'm ready for you,"croaked DeMarco, his voice like coarse gravel.

Bellucci flopped into one of the barber chairs, jerking the reclining lever until he was comfortable.

"Make yourself at home, why don't you?" croaked DeMarco begrudgingly. Bellucci ignored him and settled down to watch the game. Emilio studied the players. This was not a big-time game of cards; it was a local game, and the players were, after a fashion, all friends. But there was a depression sweeping the country, and the world. Money was scarce. This made any poker game serious. The up-all-night strain showed on the haggard Latin faces.

An hour later, Bellucci's eyes were closing; he was bored and tired. The players were all sitting on the fence. Nobody wanted to lose, and would only bet if dealt a really good hand. Bellucci knew that this was the way to play poker, but it was not for him; he liked the excitement of drawing a good card into a bad hand. To win a hand with a bluff—that was Bellucci's idea of a game of poker. Naturally, Bellucci was always broke. Through sleepy eyes and ears, he noticed a change in the tone in the game; he woke himself up in order to pay closer attention. Yes, things were heating up.

DeMarco's gravel voice croaked, "That's more like it."

He looked at his two dark cards and fingered the small amount of change that lay scattered next to the money clip with two-pound notes in it.

Corsini dealt the third card of a seven-card stud game. DeMarco liked it; he opened for a shilling, with two dark cards and a king showing. Duccio looked at his dark cards; fingering the seven of spades that was his face card, he lit a woodbine from the packet of ten in front of him, then slipped a shilling into the pot. Emilio drew the jack of hearts as his face card. Without looking at his dark cards, he threw a coin into the pot.

"I'm in."

Alonzi and Gambini put in. Corsini picked up the deck.

"Good, everybody in."

Corsini dealt a fourth card to DeMarco; it was another king.

"A pair of Kings," intoned Corsini

Corsini dealt Duccio an insignificant card. Emilio drew the ten of hearts. Alonzi and Gambini didn't improve.

"My pair of kings to bet."

DeMarco impatiently threw two half crowns into the pot.

One of them rolled round and round in diminishing loops until it lay flat on the table.

"Five shillings."

Duccio put five shillings into the pot. Emilio raised the bet.

"Your five and five more."

Bellucci was now awake, this was a poker game. He jigged the recline lever and brought himself up to a sitting position, making a screeching noise.

"Keep still or fuck off—I'm trying to play cards," growled DeMarco.

Bellucci shrugged at the barber and settled down. Alonzi and Gambini both passed and threw their cards onto the table. Corsini folded his own cards.

"I'm out," he said.

He then dealt the next cards. An ace to DeMarco, the three of clubs to Duccio, and another heart to Emilio. DeMarco was the first to speak, his croaky voice really happy.

"Nice, two kings and an ace. That will cost you a pound."

Duccio folded his cards and threw them away, making a quick sign of the cross on his forehead with his thumb. Emilio picked up his dark cards and looked at them for the first time. He put them back on the table, touching his ten and jack of hearts with a casual forefinger. Reaching into his back pocket, he fetched out two pound notes and tossed them into the pot. Emilio spoke softly in contrast to DeMarco's gravel voice.

"Your pound, and I raise you one."

DeMarco leaned forward to look at Emilio's face cards.

"Big shot. I raise you one more."

DeMarco dropped in the last pound note from his money clip.

Emilio smiled as he delved once more into his back pocket; it gave up another pound note.

"Deal, I'm in."

Corsini dealt the sixth card: another ace to DeMarco and another heart to Emilio.

"Two pairs, aces and kings. Salute, ice cream, how much you got in your pocket?" croaked DeMarco. Beads of sweat glistened on his face.

Emilio looked at his four hearts, and then at the bright ray of sunlight that slanted down from a hole in the door blind. "You bet what you like—I'm not going anywhere."

A dribble of sweat ran down DeMarco's fat face as he pondered his opponent's hand. Emilio pushed back his square shoulders and pushed his cards into a perfectly symmetrical line on the table, which made DeMarco nervous.

"Che fai? How can you be scared of me with two fat pairs?" taunted Emilio.

DeMarco reached into an inside pocket and pulled out two pound notes.

"Two pounds, I raise you two pounds."

Emilio responded, pulling five one-pound notes from a new pocket and dropping them on the table.

"I'll see you and raise you three. Corsini, deal me a good one."

Corsini looked at DeMarco for permission to deal. DeMarco snapped his fingers.

"Deal, deal."

Corsini's large sculptor's hands dwarfed the deck as he dealt a dark card to each of the players; he put the deck on the table and leant back in his chair to watch the play. DeMarco snatched up his dark card looked at it; he put it on the table, then made a show of delving into an inside pocket. He took out some folded money and dropped it on the table.

"Two pounds, I bet two pounds." Emilio picked up all his dark cards, shuffled them so that the new card came to the top, then lifted them to his face.

He squeezed them a fraction until he could see what he had drawn. Sunlight burst into the room. Scippio had opened the street door. The kid took off his cap and walked down the three steps to respectfully approach the table. Emilio didn't look up.

"Bellucci, give the boy a seat. I need him to count me some money. Here, let me feel the bag."

Scippio did as he was told. Emilio felt the weight of the moneybag. Emilio took the last two pounds from his back pocket and dropped them onto the table.

"Scippio, have we got five pounds in the bag?"

"Si, Signor Scala, more."

"Good, count it out. You can count, can't you?"

"Si, Signor Scala, I can count good."

Scippio counted the money from the bag and started making stacks of it on the table. Alonzi and Gambini went into a conference about who had what. DeMarco, face sweating, had the look of a card player who has not improved on the draw.

He stared at Emilio's hand. The four hearts looked very dangerous. Emilio only needed one heart among his three dark cards to have a jack-high flush. DeMarco picked up his three dark cards; he had not improved on two high pairs. Emilio pretended to get impatient.

"If you got the cards, trovare i soldi."

A bead of sweat trickled from DeMarco's hair line, ran down his forehead, zigzagged over the bridge of his nose, and dripped into his moustache. He looked around the faces in the room, looking for support. He found none. Feeling defeated, DeMarco picked up his cards and threw them on the table.

"It's yours, show me your flush."

Emilio started to count up the stake money.

"You have to pay to see."

Bellucci was dying with curiosity, as was the rest of the gathering.

"Emilio, go on, show him your cards, let him get something for his money."

Emilio paused from counting and flipped his three dark cards face up on the table. Two of clubs, two of spades, and the nine of diamonds. Bellucci couldn't believe it.

"Jesu Christo, you crazy bastard, a five-pound raise on a pair of twos."

Emilio unfolded DeMarco's last bet; instead of two pound notes folded together, there was only one. "DeMarco, you are a bit short on your last bet."

Emilio pushed the unfolded note in his still-shocked host's direction.

"I thought I had two pounds in that pocket, sorry." DeMarco's greasy face looked guilty.

"It's OK, accidents happen," said Emilo sarcastically, wagging his fingers in DeMarco's direction in a give-me-the-money gesture. DeMarco squirmed. Emilio enjoyed this little scenario; DeMarco was a bad loser and an even worse winner. It felt good to have fucked him for a change.

"Uno Sterlina, per favore."

Emilio wagged his finger again. DeMarco patted his pockets. He was angry for losing with a winning hand. He was embarrassed for getting caught cheating. But what really upset him was not having a pound in the till to shut Emilio up. He went over to the wall and took down a watch and chain that hung just above one of the two washbasins.

"Here, take this and be satisfied."

Emilio took the watch; the other players, enjoying the argument watched. Emilio shook the watch and listened to it, then shook it again.

"DeMarco, I saw your father give you that tin watch. It didn't work then and it doesn't work now. Give me the money."

DeMarco took back the watch and shook it. He put it to his ear. "It works, listen."

He looked around the room for support. Everybody in the room laughed, except Corsini.

"Emilio, leave him alone, he is gutted."

Emilio continued to count the pot.

"He try a cheap shot with a folded note, fuck him—it's the principle."

Bellucci thought this was getting out of hand, so he chipped in.

"DeMarco, shut up, give him one of those sweep tickets and leave it at that."

Emilio liked this suggestion.

"Yeah, give me one of those tickets, that will do."

DeMarco delved into yet another pocket and produced what used to be a book of ten sweepstake tickets, only now there was one ticket and the Stubbs of the others. He threw it on the table.

"Here, take it. Tear it out and put your name on the stub."

Emilio took the ticket and looked at it. The ticket had stamped across it in red the words 'Vendors Ticket.'

"Why this say vendors ticket?"

"'Cause I get it for free when I sell a book of tickets."

Bellucci thought Emilio was going too far and stepped in again, his fat body shaking with concealed laughter.

"Peasano, leave him alone, here's a pencil. Write your name down and let's get out of here. I need some fresh air."

Emilio wrote his name, tore off the ticket, folded it, and put it in his pocket. He then picked up his winnings and made to stand up. DeMarco wasn't yet finished. He walked back to the wall and took down a big card with the words "DEMARCO'S GRAND NATIONAL SWEEP" written across the top. Under this heading was a list of names and numbers; they ran neatly down the page one under the other, written in DeMarco's own copper-plate handwriting. He brought it back to the table.

"Emilio, aspete. Put your ticket in the sweep here with all of us. If one of us wins, all of us wins. Look! Everybody bought a ticket; they all put it in here. Corsini, Alonzi, Duccio, Cox. There's ten of us in—you will make eleven. I'll put you down on the bottom here; what's the number on your ticket?" DeMarco looked at Emilio, waiting for a reply. Emilio smiled to himself.

"I don't think so. I like a doing things on my own—you know what I mean. Come, Bellucci, Scippio, let's go."

Emilio stood up; DeMarco went back to the wall and hung the card back on its nail. The threesome said ciao to everyone, climbed the three steps, and walked out into a flood of sunshine. The tricycle was parked outside. Emilio climbed on. Scippio stood, waiting hopefully for instructions. He got them and flashed his white teeth in a broad smile. "I'll go and fill this up; meet me in the park in one hour. Bellucci, go to bed you look terrible."

Bellucci agreed and was about to waddle off. His fat legs moved into motion, but Emilio called him back. Bellucci turned; Emilio pulled five pounds from his stash.

"Here, give this to your mother; if she don't come and thank me, I will know you fucking spent it. You give it to her, OK?"

"Si, grazie Paesane, see you later."

Emilio watched his friend waddle off down the street; slowly he started to pedal the tricycle. He felt good, chuckling to himself at the image of DeMarco's face when he saw the pair of twos. Even better was the fact that he caught him trying to chisel a pound with the folded-note trick.

"The old rogue—he deserved it."

Emilio found himself singing a bit of Caruso as he parked the tricycle outside Mancini's sweet and tobacco shop. Emilio was still singing a bit of Pagliacci as he entered. Mancini looked up from the paper he was reading. "Emilio, what you so happy about?"

"I just stuffed DeMarco with a pair of twos; he had kings and aces. Give me five of those Cuban cheroots."

Mancini rummaged under the counter that was heavy with jars of striped and coloured confections. The shop had the lovely smell of cloves and aniseed and tobacco.

"How much you take off him?"

"A few quid, and a sweepstake ticket."

"Eh. The sweepstake. Vaffanculo. You, too, wanna win three hundred and fifty grand?"

"Yeah, why not? Then I can be a big shot."

Emilio put one of the cheroots in his mouth and lit it.

"You are already a big shot. I got a ticket—I'm in his pool with the boys; did you put yours in?"

"No, I keep it separate. If I win, I win."

Emilio picked up the remaining cheroots that Mancini had tightly wrapped in brown paper; he dropped a shilling on the oilcloth counter.

"Give me two pennyworth of those bonbons for the kids."

Mancini was pleased to oblige; he weighed out a quarter pound from a glass jar and poured it into a neat cone of paper. Emilio thanked the shopkeeper and left to resume his version of Pagliacci.

Emilio rode off down the street towards his yard, with thirty-six pounds in his pocket, and a ticket for the Irish sweepstake.

Emilio flicked the end of his cheroot in to the air and turned into the yard. The children climbed over him like monkeys. He pretended to have nothing for them until, under pressure, he produced the bag; holding it high over his head he made the kids jump, arms stretched up. He smiled at the tiny grasping hands until he finally gave in and gave them each a bonbon, to the little voiced cries of "Thank you, Papa!"

Emilio rode over to his wife. She was busy mixing a batch of ice cream. Slowly she turned the iron handle; Emilio could hear the mixture slurping in the barrel. He dropped the moneybag, the contents of which he had boosted with two white five-pound notes, onto the bench in front of her.

"Where have you been—it's four o'clock?"

"It was a bit slow in the park. I had to give the ice cream away"

Nazarena picked up the moneybag, weighed it in her capable hand; she sat down on a stool and poured the contents into her aproned lap. When she saw the two fivers, she looked up in surprise.

"Where you get this?"

Emilio looked sheepish, but kept on smiling.

"I've been saving up."

"Come here."

As Emilio approached, Nazarena grabbed him by the shirt and sniffed him. "Fottiti! You have been gambling. You stink like a barber shop!"

"Ah, you are too clever for me, that nose of yours will be my undoing."

Nazarena, angry but still practical, stuffed the two fivers into her special bosom pocket. Emilio laughed at his wife's serious face.

"It's all right. I won, Ok? I won."

"It's not all right. It frightens me when you gamble. I worry about the kids. What's the use of working day and night if you are going to give our money away?"

Emilio had heard all this before. He went to the mixer to test if the next batch was ready; he took of the lid and dipped in a finger. "Mmmm. Delicious."

He tried to make light of the situation. "Listen, put that money in your box; I never lose what I haven't got."

Nazarena made the sign of the cross.

"That doesn't make gambling right. I hope God, he forgive you."

Emilio refilled the tricycle, still humming Pagliacci. When he had finished, he gave his sulking wife a little hug, which she pretended to ignore. Emilio rode out of the yard.

# CHAPTER TWO

The panting fox scrabbled frantically at the base of a dry stone wall; throwing bits of earth and moss into the air it stopped quite suddenly, turning its flat, pointed head. What it saw made it defy gravity by scrambling up the stones and over the top; almost immediately, a pack of baying fox hounds followed it over in a swarm. A few stragglers stopped to reassure themselves by sniffing the stones. With a clatter of hoofs, the hunters leapt the wall to follow the hounds; twenty or so huge horses cleared the wall and the ditch beyond.

Willow Rutherford steadied her chestnut gelding, digging her left and only spur into the horse's flank. She was riding side-saddle, and urged him over the wall. The horse that took off directly behind her gained a couple of lengths in the air. The two horses landed almost together. Regaining her composure, she glanced to her right to see the mud-splattered aquiline face of Lord Dundrum.

"Super jump, Willow; we'll make a horsewoman of you yet."

They didn't jump the next ditch, as the hounds had found their fox and were busy ripping it to shreds. The master was already at the scene, as were several other huntsmen. What Willow had not been prepared for, was the cacophonic noise, the barking hounds, the shrieking horn; she could hardly make out what Lord Dundrum was saying.

"I said, damn this sweepstake; we could have run another fox." Willow smiled at him, trying to catch her breath. She patted the net that held her chestnut hair in place.

"Why can't we?"

His Lordship trotted closer, admiring the curve of her thigh across the horse's back.

"I have been asked, in my capacity as the chairman of the Hospitals Trust, to officiate at the sweepstake draw. I have to drive in to Dublin."

"Sounds like fun—can I tag along?"

Lord Dundrum contained his pleasure.

"Nothing would please me more."

They hacked the three miles back to the gatehouse of Lord Dundrum's Irish sporting estate; the house stood in a thousand acres in Kildare. The river Liffey ran through the manicured grounds. Massive mature oak trees sat by the river like ancient fortresses. Willow could see other houseguests, who hadn't fancied hunting, fishing for salmon in the gatehouse pool. The woods and bogs gave Dundrum and his friends as good a day's shooting as any estate in England.

At the gatehouse, Willow felt confident enough of her gelding to make a small wager with her host.

"Give me a start to those yew trees, and I'll race you to the house."

"You're on, and there's fifty guineas on it."

"Taken, Milord."

Willow trotted the gelding to the yew trees, gave the horse a slap with her riding crop, dug in the spur for good measure, and galloped off down the mile-long drive; Dundrum, with a thwack of his whip, gave chase.

She beat him to the house; the groom was already holding her horse when he dismounted. "I'll make a horseman of you yet," she said drily.

Dundrum laughed as the mud-spattered, beautiful Willow ran up the granite steps and into the portico door of his fine Georgian house. By the time Willow had bathed and dressed in something suitable, Dundrum was already waiting; he looked elegant, standing on the black-and-white stone floor of the hall. His chauffeur stood patiently in the drive. Beside the Rolls-Royce Phantom II, Dundrum's eyes lit up.

As Willow floated down the great marble staircase, her silver fox collared cashmere coat flapped open, revealing her silk covered breasts. Two strings of pearls swung gently between them. The shape of her long legs was evident through the soft material of her-calf length skirt. Her high heels clicking on the stone steps, Dundrum took her arm at the bottom of the stairs and guided her across the hall through the porch and into the sweet leather-scented seclusion of his motorcar. The chauffeur shut them in.

The Rolls-Royce crunched smoothly along the gravel drive. Dundrum popped the cork from a bottle Veuve Clicquot 1921, and poured it into crystal glasses. Willow was enjoying this break from London society. In fact, she was so relieved to have got away that she had hardly thought about her financial difficulties. Things were bad to say the least, with a broken engagement behind her, and her father withholding funds since her disaster in Monte Carlo. She had, at this moment, no way of paying her London gambling debts, and in a month or two she would have to refurbish her wardrobe for the summer season. Yes, she was enjoying this weekend.

The Rolls made good progress until it reached the centre of Dublin, where the roads and bridges were packed with people in festive mood. Willow watched, in amazement at the busy throng. Tinkers, hucksters selling lucky charms, mixed with a vast army of expectant-looking people, though what they were expecting, she did not know. She had seen a ticker tape parade in New York when she was a child. This was more like a gigantic fair.

"What on earth is going on?" she enquired as she looked at the spectacle from the comfort of the now-stationary car.

"It's the sweepstake draw; they've all got sweepstake fever. There has never been a lottery prize like this, ever."

The car ground to a halt, stopped by the sheer numbers of people that had crowded onto the bridge. People were trying to get a view of what was happening on the river. Dundrum opened the partition to speak to his chauffeur.

"Patrick, sound your horn and try and get to the side where we can see what's going on."

Patrick obliged, and after a few minutes had brought the Rolls up against the embankment wall. From here, it was plain to see that some kind of regatta was in progress on the river. Willow and Dundrum had a good view of what looked like a hundred jockeys, paddling small canoes with horse's heads on the front towards some winning tapes that had been stretched across the river. Behind the racing jockeys and towering into the air was a huge sixty-foot effigy, the base of which was supported by four barges. Around the effigy's neck hung a white banner with the word 'Hoodoo' printed on it. With a burst of fireworks and rockets, the effigy burst into flames. The crowd began to cheer. Willow looked on in amazement.

"What are they doing?"

"They are burning the HOODOO, an ancient ceremony believed to ward off bad luck. The Hoodoo is the king of bad luck." Dundrum looked at his watch and spoke to the chauffeur.

Ten minutes later, the Rolls pulled into the gardens of the Mansion House. Willow and Dundrum were whisked on to a dais and seated with thirty or so other dignitaries. The gardens were decked out for a garden party; bunting hung from the lampposts and several marquees twinkled with fairy lights. People were packed into every available space—thousands of them; the park was jammed.

"Thank God we're up here, out of the way."

Dundrum accepted a glass of champagne from a butler.

"Thank God, indeed. I didn't realise that this sweepstake was such a big thing."

"My dear, do you realise that over ten million tickets have been sold? You are witnessing the biggest public act of gaming since a man first threw a dice."

Willow looked about her. On a second garlanded rostrum stood a huge rotating metal drum, with a small trap door in it. Next to it was a much smaller version. Behind the drums stood two lines of immaculately starched young nurses, sixty of them in all. In front of the nurses sat a row of men; they were very excited and quite animated. She presumed that they must be the organisers. She was looking at Joe McGrath the instigator of the Sweepstake; the whole thing was his idea, and the other four men were his partners. Between them, they had organised a sales campaign that had penetrated as far afield as China, South Africa, and America. It had caused quite a stir. The Americans tried to stop ticket sales, realising that the drain of their currency by way of millions in cash being sent to Ireland had to stop. The U.S. Postal service organised legislation to permit the opening of suspicious mail, which resulted in any envelope addressed to Ireland being opened, and the money confiscated. McGrath and his team had stayed ahead of the game by organising secret agencies to collect their stake money, and nuns and priests had been used to transport suitcases of tickets across the Atlantic and to bring the cash back.

The idea of a giving a free ticket to the seller of every book of ten tickets was a fantastic idea. The world was in a depression and money was scarce; the possibility of winning half a million pounds, when a house could be bought for a couple of hundred, had proved just too much for the public to resist. McGrath and his cohorts were, at this moment, at the height of their powers.

Willow watched the McGrath camp revelling in their success, laughing and swaggering on the rostrum as the sweepstake machine wound itself up to its climax like some incredible Barnum and Bailey dream. Willow watched the five men, sensing their excitement; they were minutes away from their fortunes.

This was the moment that the millions of ticket holders around the world had been waiting for. She looked at the vast, hopeful crowd; all of them, she presumed, clutched a ticket or at least held a share in one. Dundrum took another glass of champagne from the butler. Willow put her hand on her glass, thinking.

"Explain to me how it works, who wins what?"

Dundrum took a sip.

"You see those steel drums on the rostrum? The big one holds all the Stubbs of all the tickets that have been sold—ten million, they say."

He indicated the small drum by raising his glass in its direction, and the butler filled it. "That small one holds the names of sixty horses, the proposed runners in this year's Grand National. The Nurses will each put an arm in the big drum, take out one stub, and then move on to the small drum to take out the name of one horse; eventually each nurse will hold one stub with a lucky name on it, and the name of the horse that the lucky ticket has drawn in the race. At this point, each of the sixty names pulled from the drum will instantly be entitled to a prize of two thousand pounds. Only those sixty people will be involved from then on. They will have to await the running of the Grand National in six weeks' time. The person who holds the ticket that has drawn the horse that wins the Grand National will win the first prize, close to half a million pounds. The second, two hundred thousand, and the third, one hundred and fifty thousand. The remaining fifty-seven ticket holders will have to be satisfied with the—"

Willow had got the picture, and interrupted His Lordship. "The two thousand that they have won today."

"Exactly, my dear, there you have it; quite simple, really."

Willow noticed some activity on the drum rostrum. "It seems slightly out of proportion to me. The Grand National has hundreds of horses that fall over."

"Exactly, that's what makes this such an exciting event."

Willow became thoughtful. "I think I will have another glass of champagne."

Dundrum beckoned the butler. McGrath's voice crackled over the loudspeakers; after a bit of adjustment, he could be heard loud and clear all over the gardens and by the crowd in the streets close by. One of McGrath's associates left the drum rostrum and made his way through a sort of fenced corridor that connected it to the dais that Willow and Lord Dundrum occupied. He approached Lord Dundrum. The man wore a tight-fitting suit and a bowler hat, which he raised as he spoke.

"Lord Dundrum. Will you excuse me, but we are ready for your speech, if you wouldn't mind following me."

"Yes, of course, quite ready."

Dundrum drained his glass and, taking Willow's elbow, gently ushered her to her feet. "Come along with me, you will see much more from the rostrum."

Willow and Lord Dundrum followed the man in the bowler hat through the fenced-in gangway to the rostrum. The man found Willow a seat by asking a stout middle-aged matron to vacate it.

"Shan't be long."

Lord Dundrum walked forward to the microphone. McGrath intercepted him and shook his hand. "Lord Dundrum, I will just introduce you and then leave you to it."

Dundrum had plenty of champagne in him, but he was well used to it. He looked confident as he stood next to McGrath.

"My Lords, Ladies, and Gentlemen, may I call on your attention for a few words from Lord Dundrum, Chairman of the Hospitals Trust."

McGrath handed Lord Dundrum the microphone. Looking down at the vast crowd he could feel the effect of the champagne; steadying himself he began.

"My Lords, Ladies, and Gentlemen."

Lord Dundrum's voice was lost in a roar that came from the crowd; someone had tested one of the drums by giving it a small spin. Willow could not hear what Lord Dundrum was saying, and what's more, she did not really care; she was wrestling with an idea that seemed so obvious. While her mind searched for loopholes, she saw

McGrath take the microphone and attempt to restore order; he eventually succeeded, hushing the crowd sufficiently to announce that the draw would commence.

Dundrum came back to Willow to watch McGrath spin the big drum. He turned the handle, as a man who looked like a mayor with a gold chain around his neck, spun the smaller one. The noise of the crowd dropped to a whisper, and then fell silent as the drums spun at ever-decreasing speed, gradually slowing down and then stopping. The nurses came forward to do their work. The crowd cheered as each ticket was drawn.

An hour later in a private office in the Mansion House itself, a small private party was in progress. McGrath and his partners, the Mayor of Dublin, Lord Dundrum, Willow, and no more than half a dozen other people directly connected to the sweepstake, drank champagne and congratulated each other on their brilliant success. The final figures were not available; that would take a few days. The men stood around a large baroque desk, discussing figures and the lucky characters who had drawn horses. They were going over the list to see where most of their winning tickets had been sold. More than half of them were in England, six in Ireland, ten in America, two in South Africa, and one in France. McGrath was preparing the telegrams to send to his agents, who would inform the winners.

One of his partners was preparing the press release. Apart from the sixty major winners, there were several hundred very small prizes of no real significance, except to those people who had won them; these were for people who had sold the books that had included winning tickets. There was also a secondary draw that was still in progress with hundreds of small prizes. However, the main business of the day was done.

McGrath looked up from the papers on the desk to his press agent.

"Now, listen carefully: the press are only going to get the ticket numbers, they are not to have the winners' names. And certainly not their addresses. That will be up to the individuals concerned. If they want to announce that they have drawn a horse in the sweepstake, that's up to them—have you got that, Sean?"

Sean looked up from the list to his boss.

"Got it, but the press won't like it. Can't we just give the names and hold on to the addresses?"

"No, I want the winners to be mystery-men—for a while, anyway. Let it come from them. It will make for more sustained press coverage."

Willow hovered at Dundrum's shoulder, taking everything in. She glanced at the paper with the sixty names and addresses on it and noticed that Dundrum had a copy. She moved away and took a fresh drink from a uniformed waitress, then made polite conversation with the mayor.

## CHAPTER THREE

Toby Grant was six feet tall, with smooth blond hair and a broken but not unattractive nose acquired in his youth. He sat at his desk in his opulent Piccadilly office, the neon Wrigley's chewing-gum sign that covered the facade of the building opposite flashing green and red light into the windows, making his face faintly change colour. Opposite him, in rolled-up shirtsleeves sat his wizard accountant George Lloyd, a tidy young man with a clean baby face. Toby studied an account book. Lloyd tried to lighten the proceedings.

"I'm glad they've stopped selling sweepstake tickets. It's taken thousands out of us bookmakers' pockets." Said Lloyd

Grant looked up from the book that he was studying.

"Don't worry, son, it's been good for the game; it's given everyone gambling fever—but you're right, the takings will go up now that they've stopped selling them."

Grant got back to work; he was going through the month's accounts, checking the winnings and losses of his very substantial list of punters. He turned several pages in the ledger, which brought him to the bad debts page; he gave Lloyd a string of instructions on how to deal with the various non-payers. These ranged from sending his two henchmen, Snowy and Ginger, to deal with severe cases, or cutting off the credit of marginal offenders. He came eventually to a name that he did not recognise.

"Who is this Mr. Rutherford who owes us four grand?"

Lloyd looked across at his boss.

"He is a she, Mr. Grant; she's a friend of Lord St. Ledger. Her father makes Rutherford Tractors—he's blinding rich." Grant closed the book.

"Then why hasn't she paid? She's owed the money for over eight weeks."

Lloyd did not like getting roasted by his boss; he cleared his throat

"I don't know, Mr. Grant."

"Don't know. Well, find out, get hold of her. I'll talk to her."

"I have left loads of messages; she is, apparently, away." Grant got up and walked to the window, looking out over Piccadilly Circus.

"I didn't get here by letting people knock me for grands, and I don't intend to start now. Get hold of her, Ok?"

Grant put on his jacket and left the office. Lloyd sat in the flashing neon light and started making phone calls.

CHAPTER FOUR

Willow returned from Ireland the next morning to find a pile of bills, no letter from her father; a string of phone messages, mostly from men that she didn't like, one from Lord St. Ledger, whom she did like, and several from Toby Grant's office. She wasted no time, asking her maid to run her bath, choosing an outfit that would kill, and preparing herself to make an impression on her bookmaker.

Grant was working in the office with Lloyd when his secretary announced that there was a Miss Rutherford to see him. He dismissed Lloyd and went to his mirrored drinks cabinet; looking at his reflection in the glass, he put on his jacket and knotted his tie. Then he gave his hair a couple of flicks with a tortoise-shell comb that he always carried. When he felt ready to receive, he opened the office door.

"Miss Rutherford."

Willow was looking at the array of sporting photographs that covered the walls of the reception-come-secretary's office; she turned and swished past Grant, chiffon and scent leaving a trail behind her. Grant stood, transfixed for a moment. She was gorgeous. Willow noticed the effect her entrance had made on the man. She went to the window. Grant finally closed the door.

"So, this is the den of the famous Toby Grant. My friend Lord St. Ledger bets with you."

Toby found his voice.

"Bunkie St.Ledger—yes, he has been known to indulge in the odd wager. Toby Grant at your service, Miss—it is Miss Rutherford?"

"I'm afraid so. Can't seem to catch a husband."

Toby looked at the beautiful woman before him. He could think of a number of ways that she could settle her debt. Toby offered her a chair; she accepted, lowered herself into it, and crossed her long legs. Toby tried hard not to look as he walked around the desk and dropped into his seat.

"Smoke?"

He lifted the lid of a ghastly onyx cigarette box and pushed it towards her.

"No thanks, Toby. I don't smoke. Gambling is my vice. I returned from Ireland this morning and found so many messages from your office, I thought I should come and see you."

Toby was glad she had.

"Over-enthusiastic staff, I'll have a word with them."

Toby lit a cigarette.

"Toby, I'll come to the point. I can't pay you. Not right now, anyway."

Toby leaned back in his chair, making the most of this advantage. "You're supposed to be a very wealthy girl."

Willow turned her head to look at a picture in a nonchalant gesture. "My father is; in fact, he's stinking. Black sheep, I'm afraid."

She swung her head back to look at him and gave him a fatal little smile. "I haven't come to beg for mercy; you will get paid, one way or another."

Toby put his hands together. "That's very reassuring."

Willow re-crossed her legs and looked him squarely in the eyes. "Look, I don't know how to ask this, so I'll go ahead any way. Would you like to make a lot of money?"

She looked directly into Toby's eyes.

"I love making lots of money."

Toby looked at his watch; he had his confidence now. "I make it about lunch time. Shall we discuss this over a bite? Soho is just around the corner."

Willow made an instant decision to keep this man at bay, at least until he had taken the bait—that is, if he was going to take the bait.

"Let's talk business in the office. If you like what you hear, I'd be delighted to have lunch with you."

Toby looked a little put out; on the other hand, he felt he was pushing his luck, so he did not take the rejection badly. "Suit yourself. I'd like to take you to lunch, anyway, if only to discuss the one way or another that you mentioned earlier."

Toby spoke with a tone intended to remind Willow that she owed him money that she was not in a position to immediately repay. Willow took the hint; it served to remind her that she was dealing with a successful and very hard man.

She threw him her best smile as she produced a piece of folded paper from her small snakeskin clip bag and handed it to Toby.

"This is a list of the names and addresses of the sixty people who have drawn Grand National runners in the Irish Sweepstake. The draw was made last night; this information has not been made public."

Toby looked at the list. "So?"

"So! Mr. Grant, three of the names on that list will win the biggest prize in history; this is the first sweepstake of this size, and I believe there is an administrative loophole."

Toby smiled; he liked this girl, she had balls. He could work with her if the idea was any good. "Loophole?"

Toby had left his seat at the prospect of lunch with Willow but seated himself again, putting his elbows on his desk. "Tell me about this loophole."

Willow leaned forward on her chair and, reaching provocatively, took the sheet of paper from Toby's hand.

"Each of these names has won two thousand pounds, because they drew a horse in the race. Whoever has drawn the winner will pick up approximately three hundred and fifty thousand pounds, the second two hundred thousand, and the third one hundred and fifty. The losers will get nothing. I believe that we can sell these people some very expensive insurance."

Willow paused to read Toby's reaction.

"Well go on," he said, a little impatiently.

"If we move fast, I think we can buy substantial shares in all these tickets for a price far lower than the amount that we would be sure to win. Toby, look, the Grand National itself is a lottery. Last year, nineteen horses fell. If you had drawn one of these tickets, I know you would want to hedge your bet by selling a part of it, and you are a bookie. Most of these people are ordinary folk. The two thousand they have won for drawing a horse is a fortune to them. We are in a depression; if we guarantee these people—let's say, a further two thousand for half, or a third of their ticket—they would be crazy not to except. The reason this works is that the prize is so astronomically out of proportion to the risk involved. To these people, even half of a prize this size is an absolute fortune."

Toby rubbed the bridge of his nose with a forefinger. 'This crazy idea almost works,'; he thought to himself.

"Wouldn't we have to spend almost as much as we stand to win?"

Willow adjusted her position in the chair.

"That's just it—we wouldn't. Firstly, not all the sixty horses will run; there are new restrictions in place this year. By the time of the race, the field will probably be reduced to less than fifty runners. So we start budgeting at that figure. Let's say for half of an outsider's ticket, we have to pay two grand. For the more fancied runners, will have to pay a bit more, and for the favourites a bit more again—but you can believe me every one of those names will have a price. If we buy half tickets of all the runners, we are guaranteed to collect half of all the prize money, and our share would total three hundred and twenty-five thousand pounds. If we had to spend two hundred grand to achieve that, we are still guaranteed to make one hundred and twenty-five thousand. It's fool proof."

Toby did a bit of mathematics on a pad, then looked up at Willow. "It's not a bad scam—that is, if we can buy all the tickets."

Willow came straight back at him, sensing that she had him hooked. "Look there's something else; at least ten of the horses are no hopers, and will only get placed if there are a lot of fallers. Rather than buy shares in those tickets, we can buy the horses; they aren't worth more than five hundred pounds apiece. Having done that, we can scratch them, make sure they don't run."

Toby laughed. "You are a naughty girl, Willow. That's cheating."

"Yes, I suppose it is."

They both laughed. Toby got up from the desk and went to the bar.

"Drink?"

"Only if you have champagne"

Toby did have champagne; he brought a bottle from the bar with two glasses, popped the cork, and poured. "Why me?"

Willow sipped her drink. "I owe you money, for one thing, and you're the only man I know who would understand this deal; you've got the money, and the guts."

Toby was flattered, and mesmerised by the cool charm of this young beauty. "What do you want out of it?"

Willow thought for a moment; she looked into Toby's eyes. "Twenty percent of the profits, and you write off my debt."

Toby walked to the door of his office and opened it; he peered out, and. Willow heard him ask Polly his secretary, "Get George Lloyd up here."

Toby closed the door and sipped his drink.

"I'll tell you what I'm going to do with you—I'm going to introduce you to my accountant and right-hand man. You sit down with him and work out the accurate details—a feasibility study, if you like. If he likes it and then I like the work you've both done, I'll give your scheme serious consideration."

George Lloyd entered the office, knocking first but not waiting for a reply. Toby put his glass down. "George Lloyd, Willow Rutherford, you are going to do a bit of work together."

George walked over to Willow and shook her hand.

"We've met, but only on the telephone. It was me who opened your account."

Willow gripped his hand and hit him with a smile.

"Now, Willow, perhaps you will join us both for a bit of lunch."

Toby turned to George. "Ask Polly to book a table for three at the Romanoff."

George did as he was told. Toby took hold of the back of Willow's chair. "Do you like fish, Willow?"

# CHAPTER FIVE

Emilio rode his tricycle around the park; he had been on the move since nine o'clock. It was now twelve, and not a good day to sell ice cream. The sky was overcast and frowned down on him. A cold wind came off the river—removing, he was sure, any craving that even his most loyal customers might have for an ice cream. He had done his best to do a bit of business, but the weather was against him. He thought about riding over to DeMarco's to hustle up a game of cards, but he couldn't do that; he had no cash and wouldn't have until he paid off the money he had borrowed to buy the tables and chairs and other things his wife had ordered to make a small café out of the shed in the yard they rented under the railway bridge. He cursed the wind; he had taken one shilling all day.

He rode from the lake to the zoo entrance; the zoo was always good for a few customers at lunchtime. He sat there for a few minutes, ringing his bell to no avail. He saw his eldest son, Joe, running across the park. Joe reached his father, puffing and out of breath; the boy suffered from asthma, but the brave kid constantly pushed himself to run and play like other boys.

"Papa, Papa, Mamma sent me. There is a man come to find you, and he is waiting in the café."

Emilio looked at the earnest little face of his eldest boy. "What man is that, Joe?"

Joe climbed on to the back of the tricycle. "I don't know, Papa. He has a black suit and a bowler hat and a black bag. He's been waiting a long time."

"OK, we go, hold on tight."

Emilio rode across the park, wondering if he was in trouble. Some of the Italians had been having problems with the immigration people. Maybe they turned down his application to be a British citizen. Maybe the man was a policeman; Emilio hoped this had nothing to do with the two barrels of wine that he was looking after for Bellucci. With apprehension, he parked the tricycle in the yard. Joe jumped off and raced in to the little café to tell his mother that Papa was coming. Emilio followed him in. There were about a dozen regular customers drinking tea from thick mugs; Emilio knew them all. Nazarena was behind the makeshift counter.

Sitting at a small table in the corner was the man in a black suit. Nazarena saw Emilio and indicated to the man; she looked worried, and she hated and mistrusted any dealings with officialdom.

"He's been a waiting for a long time. You go and talk to him; I will bring some coffee."

Emilio pulled out a chair and sat down. As he did so, the man stood up. "Mr. Emilio Scala?" Emilio looked up. The man held out his hand. "John Carter, from Weatherby and Nash solicitors. May I sit down?"

Emilio took the man's hand and shook it with a strong workingman's grip.

Carter sat down in his chair, still gripped in Emilio's hand.

"Si, si, I am Emilio Scala."

Carter freed his hand. "Would you mind showing me some proof—a passport or something?"

Emilio was now paranoid. "Look, mister, me and my family are legal, completely legal. What do you want me for?"

Carter looked embarrassed. 'This man has the wrong end of the stick,' he thought. He took off his hat; it left a groove in his hair that ran all the way around his skull.

"No, no, Mr. Scala, I don't want you for anything; I have something for you. But I must have proof that you are him."

Carter laughed at his own joke. Emilio still had not understood. His spine tingled; he sensed that something serious was going on. With some apprehension, he looked at his wife.

"Nazarena, bring me my passport."

Nazarena rummaged under the counter and brought out a tin box. She took a key that was attached to her under skirt with a safety pin and unlocked the box. She took out the Scala family papers, all tied up in a ribbon. She put them on a tray with two cups of coffee, and took it to the table.

By this time, the customers were all ears and eyes. Local working people, a couple of labourers, Jimmy the newspaper vendor, Terry Cox the milkman—all tuned into the conversation. Emilio picked the bundle off the tray and undid it; he sorted through the papers, eventually flourishing his passport to Mr. Carter.

"Here. My passport, completely legal."

Carter took it flipped the pages, taking his time to read it. "That looks in order. One more question—do you have a ticket for the Irish Sweepstake?"

At the word 'sweepstake', all ears in the little café pricked up.

"Si, si I have a ticket."

Emilio stood up and went behind the counter to a small picture of the Madonna that hung on a nail. He reached behind it and retrieved the sweepstake ticket from where he had hidden it six weeks before. He unfolded it and took it back to Carter.

"Here, you see? My ticket."

Emilio's hand trembled slightly as he held it out. Carter took the ticket and compared it to a piece of paper in his brief case. "Mr. Scala, you have drawn a horse in the Grand National. You've drawn Grakle."

Emilio went a little pale as Carter's words sunk into his shocked mind. "I win the Sweepstake?"

Carter smiled. "No, you have not won the Sweepstake. But you have drawn a horse, and you have won two thousand pounds, and a chance to win the Sweepstake."

Emilio sat down; he actually looked sad, as if about to cry. Then his expression changed almost immediately to one of joy as he jumped up from the table, spilling the coffee. "Nazarena! Vieni qua! This man he says I win the Sweepstake! Due mille sterline, due mille sterline!"

The customers, no longer interested in their tea mugs, started babbling to each other. Jimmy the newspaper boy ran out of the café to start the grapevine. Terry Cox the milkman was one of DeMarco's customers and had a ticket in the barber's pool; he wanted more information. Emilio picked up Nazarena and spun her around; Joe and the other Kids who had been watching from the door picked up the infectious activity, and the noise frightened the toddler, who started to cry loudly. Nazarena, embarrassed by the impromptu dance, freed herself from Emilio's bear hug and picked up the screaming baby, soothing it immediately; the place was a madhouse. Within minutes, people were crowding into the café. Bellucci came in, and as Emilio's friend could see the situation getting out of hand. He took control. The fat man stood, clapping his chubby hands.

"Aspete, aspete. Listen, you all go bloody crazy." He clapped his hands again. "Listen, everybody, give Emilio some peace; everybody, the café is closed, come back later on." He used his weight to usher most of the customers out. "Don't worry about paying, it's all on the house."

He gently pushed a couple more characters out through the door. Terry Cox was still trying to find out if this stroke of good fortune affected him in any way and was praying to God that Emilio was in the DeMarco sweep with all the other Italians. He came face-to-face with Bellucci.

"Mr. Bellucci, is that ticket in DeMarco's pool?"

Bellucci grabbed him gently. "I don't know, ask DeMarco."

Bellucci pushed the milkman through the door. Now the place was empty except for Emilio, Nazarena, Mr. Carter, Bellucci, and the kids. He locked the door. Emilio was still in shock; after his initial reaction he had sat down, stunned.

He was brought out of his shock by his son Joe, who came over to his father, thinking that he was upset. He put his little arm around his papa's neck. "What's wrong, Papa, what's wrong?"

Emilio took his hands from his face and looked at the boy. "Nothing is wrong, son. We are very lucky, very lucky."

Joe held on to his Papa. "That's because Mamma always says her prayers. Isn't it, Papa?"

Emilio hugged him. "Yes, son, that's right. That's right."

Emilio turned to Bellucci, who was at the window telling the crowd in an animated mime to go away and come back later. "Bellucci, vino. Bring a jug of that vino of yours from the yard, subito! Lets celebrate."

Mr Carter had sat; watching the confusion and the chaos of this celebrating family, he felt good about being the harbinger of good news. So often in his job, he was the man with the bad. He saw that Emilio had calmed down sufficiently to continue his business and called him over. "Mr Scala, here is my card. If you call at my office at eleven tomorrow with your ticket, you may pick up your cheque."

Emilio took the card. "Si, si, eleven o'clock. Thank you, thank you. Stay and drink some wine with us."

Carter refused politely; he had more work to do. Emilio thanked him again and had Joe show him out the back way through the yard.

Nazarena had rocked the toddler to sleep. She had understood very little of what had been going on, having no knowledge of the ticket— or for that matter, the Irish Sweepstake. "Now, you come here and you tell me what's going on."

Emilio knew this was going to be a tough one. He had sworn that he would not gamble, at least until the debts were paid. "Look, I win a ticket in the lotteria, and I win."

Nazarena felt betrayed. Her husband had sworn on the Bible that he would not gamble. "You liar, you are a liar."

She crossed herself, snatched up the toddler, and stormed out the back of the café, leaving Emilio staring at Bellucci in disbelief. He had won two thousand pounds and his wife was holding him to a gambling promise. "Mannaggia!," he swore to himself. "I will never understand women."

Bellucci poured a couple of glasses of wine. Now at last, the two men could sit down and discuss the pros and cons of such good fortune.

# CHAPTER SIX

The next morning, Emilio and Bellucci dressed in their church suits and left Battersea by bus. At eleven sharp, they entered the West End offices of Weatherby and Nash, where to their delight and relief they realised that they were not dreaming or being conned. Mr. Carter gave them the cheque: two thousand pounds.

Bellucci wanted to hold it, he put it in his pocket, took it out again, rustled it, kissed it. Eventually Emilio took it away from him after thanking Mr. Carter as if he had personally given them the money.

They left Carter's office to walk the streets of London's West End. Emilio wanted to open a bank account with the money. Bellucci agreed.

"Any bank would be proud to have such a sum to look after," Emilio agreed. They spent some time looking for a bank that pleased them, choosing Coutts in Piccadilly for no other reason than the amount of carved Italian marble on the facade. Emilio approached the liveried doorman.

"Excuse me, I win the sweepstake and I want to put my money in your bank."

The towering doorman looked down with a bemused smile. "Certainly, sir, if you would like to go through the bank to the central desk and ask to speak to Mr. Travers-Brown."

Emilio and Bellucci strolled into the vaulted splendour of the impressive building. All the staff appeared to be men in morning suits; Bellucci thought this was strange. "They all look like undertakers in here."

Emilio had the answer. "That's how big shots do their business."

They approached the central desk; one of the morning-suited men intercepted them. "Can I help you, sir?"

Emilio puffed out his chest. "Yes, I win some money on the Sweepstake and I like to put it in your bank."

The clerk put his fingers together in subconscious supplication. "Yes, sir. May I ask you who has introduced you to us?"

Emilio looked at the clerk blankly. "Introduced?"

The clerk asked again, "Yes, sir, your references."

Emilio didn't understand.

"You need to have references to open an account here at Coutts. Do you have any?"

Bellucci could see there was a problem. "This place is for big shots. They do not want our money. Come on, let us go."

Emilio motioned him to be quiet. "You don't want my money?"

The clerk was a bit stumped with this question. "Yes, sir, but you must have references."

Emilio had had enough of this. "You gonna be sorry when I win that big prize. I will put my money somewhere else."

The clerk stayed calm. "Ah, thank you, sir.."

Emilio and Bellucci walked out.

"I told you the place is a funeral parlour. There is a Lloyds bank across the road; my mother cashed a cheque in one of them once. They would like to look after your money."

The man at Lloyd's was very helpful. He opened the account immediately and gave Emilio a chequebook. Thus armed, Emilio and Bellucci sauntered through the Burlington Arcade, feeling like a couple of toffs. The two cigars they bought at Sullivan's helped the illusion.

Emilio loved Soho. He had come here every Christmas since he came to England, bringing Nazarena and their limited budget to buy all the bits and pieces to celebrate with a traditional Italian meal. On these occasions, they would only shop at the food and wine emporium of Signor Bianchi. Bellucci had never been to Soho; just the name conjured up the taste of salami, prosciutto, mortadella, and other delicious things that the fat man often craved. He was not to be disappointed.

Emilio led the way. They passed a huge sturgeon that lay on trays of ice outside Romanoff's Russian restaurant. They passed Mr. Chin, the Chinese cook with strings of toffee-covered ducks hanging from poles. Bellucci was impressed with Emilio's knowledge of this almost foreign city.

"You smell that?" Bellucci sniffed the air. "That's DeSilva's coffee shop. Three hundred kinds he has."

Bellucci sniffed again. "I can smell all of them, mmm."

They went in and bought a pound of dark mocha beans as a present for Bellucci's mother. On the corner of Greek Street and Old Compton Street, they found Bianchi's.

"What a place," whispered Bellucci as he looked through the window. The incredible colourful display made his mouth water. Emilio led the way over the terrazzo floor, liberally sprinkled with sawdust. An assistant in a long green apron offered to help them.

"Tell Bianchi that Scala would like to speak to him."

The assistant didn't have to move. Bianchi, sitting on his stool at the back of the shop, heard every word uttered within his portals. He straitened his waistcoat, climbed off his stool, and walked with tiny steps into the shop.

"Emilio, you lucky man, everybody hear you win the Sweepstake." Bianchi gave Emilio a bear hug.

"This is my friend Bellucci. We come to buy my wife all the things she misses from Italy. We wanna big box. Emilio pointed to a large wicker hamper.

"Si, si, no problem." Bianchi clapped his hands, attracting the attention of an assistant. The tasting began immediately. Bellucci started on the salami; there were so many kinds that he had to resort to tasting—a slice of this a slice of that. He was in heaven.

Emilio was more restrained; he knew what he wanted. A stone flagon of virgin olive oil. A jet-black smoked ham from Tuscany. A huge Parmesan cheese, tins of anchovies, sardines in olive oil, a case of tinned tomatoes, a sack of durum flower to make pasta, packets of dried mushrooms. Bellucci had progressed to the Mortadella; Emilio selected several boxes of sweet torrone and packets of almonds. As he moved over to the wine shelves, he ordered a case of Chianti in its straw-clad bottles. The spree continued until the huge hamper groaned.

Finally, Bianchi returned to his stool to total the bill. He sat talking to himself. "Eight pounds of salami, one whole ham, one four-pound Prosciutto, a flagon of olive oil. . ." etc., etc.

He finished his addition and called Emilio over. "I make it twenty-three pounds and seven shillings, is that OK?"

Emilio wrote his first check. Bianchi took a bottle of Grappa from a shelf and wrapped it in brown paper; he pressed it into Emilio's hand. "Un regalo per te."

Emilio thanked Bianchi as he walked them to the door. Outside the shop, the Bianchi delivery cart stood at the curb. Its single horse pushed its nose bag around the gutter, trying to get its tongue into the corners. Bianchi's assistants struggled to get the huge hamper onto the cart.

An hour later, Emilio and Bellucci sat on the back of the Bianchi cart, legs dangling, swigging from the bottle of Grappa as they crossed Vauxhall Bridge on their way to Nazarena's kitchen.

Nazarena heard the horse and cart clatter over the cobblestones of the yard. She was in the scullery of what used to be a one-up, one-down porter's cottage, tucked against the brickwork of the railway viaduct at the back of the cobbled yard. Carrying her baby, she came out to see what was going on. To her surprise, she found Emilio and Bellucci, quite drunk, sitting on the back of Bianchi's wagon.

Emilio jumped off. "It's OK everything is OK." He hoped to prevent her inevitable tirade for finding them pissed. He took off his jacket. "Here, hold this, we have something for you."

Nazarena took the jacket and watched as the driver, Bellucci, and Emilio manhandled the hamper off the wagon.

"This, my wife, is for you." Emilio theatrically opened the lid.

Nazarena's face lit up at the sight of so many lovely things. With the toddler tightly gripped in her left arm, she reached into the hamper for a preliminary sort through the merchandise. From the corner of her eye, she saw Bellucci stagger and trip; she then noticed that Emilio was a little unsteady on his feet. "You're drunk, the both of you."

She made a sign of the cross, closed the lid of the hamper, and quickly walked back into the cottage. The men followed, dragging the hamper.

"Emilio! She will be all right when she unpacks this lot."

With a tug, Emilio got the hamper moving; the other two pushed.

"I know. Let's get it inside; I wanna see her face."

The men manhandled the hamper through the scullery door. Nazarena had given up her pretence at anger, having been overcome with curiosity. In fact, she was ready with a large blue coffee pot. "Sit down, all of you, drink some black coffee."

She lifted the two-third's empty Grappa bottle from Bellucci's pocket and put it on the table and took the deliveryman by the arm. "Come sit down, have some coffee."

The boys, Joe and Freddy, came in from the street, and pretty soon the table was buzzing. Fresh bread was sliced into thick chunks, and a salami with the end thinly sliced was dived on by the children; for a change, Bellucci bided his time—he felt a little ill. Nazarena had hurriedly set the table and now got on with the business of unpacking the hamper. Young Joe helped her put the supplies away and hang things up on the hooks in the pantry cupboard.

Emilio dipped a chunk of bread in to olive oil on a plate. "If I win the sweepstake, I'm gonna make a cafeteria like a fairy land—all pink mirrors and neon lights, like in America."

Nazarena, who was eavesdropping, made another sign of the cross and whispered, "Please, God," and then groaned a long "Mmmmm."

As she discovered the black smoked ham, she hung it from a hook. "I love you, you are such a dreamer," she said as she sorted through the goodies.

Bellucci poured another cup of coffee. "Have you seen DeMarco? They say he has gone crazy."

Emilio looked up from the olive oil plate. "What do you mean, gone crazy?"

Bellucci sensed danger; Emilio had acted strange at the mention of DeMarco's name. He changed the subject. There was already enough aggravation in the ghetto with the guys from DeMarco's; best to let Emilio sort them out.

"You can sell a bit of your ticket, you know. You could get a few grand for half of your ticket. Then if Grakle falls over, you still get plenty money."

Emilio looked round to see if his wife was listening. "I've thought about it. But wouldn't it be really something to win a pot like that?"

Bellucci leaned across the table. "You're fucking crazy. Trust in God, but tie up your donkey first."

Emilio brought his face close to Bellucci's. "Grakle aint no donkey."

"And you are not God!" came the fat man's reply. "If you don't sell a bit, and that fucking horse falls over, she will kill you."

Emilio took a sip of coffee and muttered under his breath, "Madonna."

# CHAPTER SEVEN

Willow had spent most of the day working with George Lloyd, going over all the pros and cons that they could foresee. They had discussed ways of buying the cheaper horses, and found a way to do so without raising suspicion.

George, as a major bookmaker, had many contacts in the racing game, and naturally he had a list of bent trainers, jockeys, and a little team that the firm used in dire circumstances to dope the odd dangerous horse. They would also need the services of a first-class international lawyer to help make the deals with the ticket holders. Willow knew just the man, Justin Freedman, head of one of the biggest firms in London. She agreed to visit him later.

Willow was confident that she had won George over. At first he had been sceptical, but as she shot away his arguments, his confidence had grown, and then she had noticed greed take over as George started to throw ideas of his own into the plot. "I've got a man who can make any but the most well-protected horse in the country go lame."

Willow loved it. George was in. They took the results of their labours upstairs to Grant's office. He was in a jovial mood as they entered.

"I've just had the most amazing coincidence. My cousin David has just called me from Atlantic City; he's an accountant to the mob. He tells me that Capone is in on the sweepstake. Apparently they forged thousands of sweepstake tickets. The punters who bought the forgeries will never know they're duds, because the counterfoils never got to the draw. Brilliant; we aren't the only ones trying to work the Sweepstake."

Willow was slightly embarrassed as she heard George butt in. "With respect, Mr. Grant, what they have done is illegal. Miss Rutherford's idea is much cleverer than that."

Toby looked at his number-one employee. "Oh, you like her idea then, do you?"

"I do, Mr. Grant. There's a lot of work to be done, but I think we can make a lot of money."

Willow gave a smile of satisfaction. "Thank you, George. Shall we show Toby our plans?"

Grant motioned them to his desk. "Let's see what you've got."

George laid a file on the table and took a seat. Willow walked around the desk and sat herself next to Toby.

"Since we first talked, quite a few horses have dropped out. This makes our job a lot easier. As of today, there are forty-three runners. Out of those, there are fifteen doubtful creatures, including the horses that we will buy cheap, and those that we can get at."

George opened his file. "If we exclude them, that leaves us with twenty-eight tickets to secure."

He passed Grant a list of names. Grant took the list. "How do we work out what to offer these people?"

Willow leaned across Grant to point to a name on the list. "It's fairly arbitrary. We just have to work on their fear of losing, make them feel secure. What we offer will have to be linked directly to the anti-post price of each horse. We should be prepared to pay more for the fancied runners and correspondingly less for the outsiders. We will make them an offer well within our budget. If they refuse, we negotiate. Our aim is to acquire all the tickets for an average price of five thousand pounds; we may have to go as high as ten for the really fancied runners, but a person who has drawn a hundred-to-one shot will be happy to take a grand. Remember, he gets to keep a third of any winnings. He will, as it were, be insured. He has two thousand for drawing the horse, plus whatever we pay him, which means he has guaranteed pay-out, even if his horse falls over. If, however, it should win or be placed, he will still receive a third of the prize, a fortune."

Grant dropped the sheet of paper on the desk.

"So how much do we have to invest?"

George had the answer. "If we can buy a three-quarter share in all twenty-eight tickets for an average of five grand, one hundred and forty thousand pounds. Our return should be three quarters of the total prize money, four hundred and fifty thousand pounds; take out our one hundred and forty invested, and we make three hundred and ten grand profit."

Grant liked this result, but he had another question. "What happens if we can't acquire a share in all the tickets?"

George looked at Willow. "Well. Any ticket that we can't acquire, we would have to see to it that that horse does not run, or at least can't win."

Grant smiled at Willow. "I've already told you, you are a very naughty girl."

Willow reacted by pulling an innocent face. Grant thought for a moment, rubbing his hands. "All right, I like it. I will make the cash available. You are going to need a team. An international lawyer, for a start."

"Willow has that covered; she's going to see him this afternoon." "Is he any good; can he be trusted?" Grant enquired.

"Oh, yes, Toby, he is a very good friend," said Willow with a knowing smile.

Toby went to his safe and took out four bank-wrapped bundles of cash. "Give this to the lawyer; we will want his people to buy the foreign tickets."

Willow took the bundles. "I'll need a bigger hand bag."

# CHAPTER EIGHT

George Lloyd spotted Sidi Tucker propping up the bar in the King's Head in Mayfair. Sidi Tucker had been a vet in his youth, but he had been struck off years ago. Now he made a living as a professional nobbler; he was the best.

"How is Mr. Grant?" he said as he raised the pint of bass to his thin lips.

"He's well," said George Lloyd, slipping Sidi a fat envelope.

"I had better have a look at the list now. You know there are some yards I can't get near."

George took a piece of paper from his pocket; Sidi took it and studied it. "I reckon I can do eight of those."

He took a stubby pencil from a pocket and made circles around eight of the names. "If I get 'em all done, there will be a bonus?"

"Absolutely, Sidi. Mr. Grant appreciates a job well done."

Over the next week, Sidi toured England, travelling in his Morris Tourer. He paid some of the money that George Lloyd had given him to bent grooms in four of the yards on his list. The other four, he visited himself.

Sidi knew the yard of Mickey Morris very well; he had visited it as a vet many times. In pouring rain, he parked his car in a thick wood and walked the four miles cross-country to the yard, carrying a sack.

Mickey Morris was a farmer. He trained for himself on his own farm. There were six looseboxes situated a hundred and fifty yards from the house. Between the looseboxes and the house was a kitchen garden, flanked by a dry stone wall, against which leaned a wooden chicken coop with a partially covered wire run.

Creeping like the expert poacher he was, Sidi got into position behind the dry stone wall; from here he had a clear view of the boxes. Above the boxes was a long room with a slated roof; a wooden staircase ran up the side of a building. Sidi knew that two grooms slept in that room. The rain pelted down. Greystoke, eighth in the betting of the Grand National, would be in the double corner box.

All was quiet in the yard. The house lights were out. The dog would be in its kennel, sheltering from the rain, though this wouldn't stop it making a racket if it got a sniff of trouble. Sidi slowly made his wet way along the back of the wall until he stood directly behind the chicken run. Reaching into the sack, he grabbed the neck of a young vixen. He threw it high into the air over the wall into the partially covered chicken run. It landed with a clatter on a metal chicken feeder. As Sidi ran back along the wall, the dog barked and leapt from its kennel, charging across the kitchen garden to bark furiously at the trapped, panic-stricken fox.

By the time Sidi had got to the end of the wall close to the corner box, lights came on in the house. At the same time, the door at the top of the wooden groom's staircase opened. Sidi hopped the wall, let himself into the corner box, took a hammer from his pocket, and gave one firm crack to the Tendon Extensor Metacarpi Magnus of Greystokes near foreleg. He let himself out of the box, slipped into the shadows along the wall, and jumped over.

Glancing back at the yard, he saw the commotion at the chicken run. The frenzied dog was still barking loudly at the terrified fox. The two partially dressed wet grooms egged him on. Sidi saw the light from the open farmhouse door; he was well on his way into the woods when he heard the shot from the 12-gauge bore that killed the fox.

Sidi drove his car through the night, and arrived at his next target: the yard of Graham Bell, trainer of the eight-year-old chaser, Easter Hero. He parked his car a mile from the yard. His watch stood at four a.m.. Sidi made his stealthy way cross-country. Dawn was an hour away as Sidi crawled along a culvert that ran between Graham Bell's stables and the back end of Doncaster racecourse.

All was quiet in the yard, but Sidi had a problem: he didn't have an intimate knowledge of this yard, and would therefore have to use a random approach to find his target amongst the eight horses in training; he had no way of telling where Easter Hero was.

From the cover of a hedgerow, Sidi could see the yard clearly. Twenty feet from him was a stone water trough. From the big pocket of his poacher's coat, he took a muslin bag, which contained a pound of powder of his own preparation. A pound was sufficient to contaminate eighty gallons of water.

Sidi crawled on his belly to the trough and tipped it in; crouching low, he reached up and over, giving the water in the trough a stir with his hand; then, retracing his steps, he rested in the culvert for a few moments. Nothing stirred.

He made his way back to his car and drove away.

As dawn was about to break, Graham Bell's head lad led Easter Hero from his box to prepare him for some road work, past the water trough. His cye caught a glimpse of something glinting in the water; closer inspection revealed the upturned bellies of five dead gold fish.

Graham, being the canny old  trainer he was, kept the fish in the horse's water as a gauge to its purity, as his father had done before him, though Sidi hadn't known this.

On hearing his name, Graham Bell stormed across the yard; one glance at the belly-up fish gave him a sense of satisfaction. At least the old trick worked. "Have any of the animals been watered?" he asked impatiently.

"No, sir. I was just passing when I saw the fish."

"That's good." He dipped his hand in the trough, then smelt his fingers. "You see, lads, it pays to be vigilant; someone has tried to do in Easter Hero. Drain this trough and wash it out. You aren't to leave that horse's side 'till the race is over."

The next morning, Greystokes was pronounced lame and scratched from the National. Easter Hero wasn't.

# CHAPTER NINE

Emilio sat in his scullery; once again, he was under extreme pressure from Nazarena on the subject of his gambling. She had always looked after the family money. That was, when she could get her hands on it. The problem now was that she didn't understand this bank account business. The chequebook mystified her; she could barely write her name. As far as she was concerned, Emilio had nearly two thousand pounds at his disposal—a very dangerous situation, and one, from experience, that she was not about to tolerate.

"You show me how to do this cheque book. I always look after the money; you are no good with money. You gamble."

Emilio suffered under the onslaught. "Listen, this is real money. It's not like a five-pound note that you can stick in your vest pocket."

Nazarena wasn't having it. "You give me the check book, I take care of it." She snatched the book, stuffed it into her vest pocket, and continued her ironing.

"Okay. But not another word about my gambling; that's men's business."

Emilio was saved from any more of this by the voice of Bellucci shouting through the window. "Emilio, vieni qua!. I wanna talk to you."

Emilio put on his jacket and went out the door, leaving Nazarena to pat her breast pocket in victory.

In the yard, Bellucci grabbed Emilio's arm and led him out of earshot of the cottage. "You've got the big shot today. There is someone wants to see you. There is a big car, with a girl in the back. A beautiful girl."

The twosome rounded the corner to find Grant's big shining red Talbot Tourer. As they approached, the door opened and Willow's long legs swung out onto the running board. She stepped down onto the pavement. "Mr. Scala, can I have a word with you?"

Emilio looked her up and down. Bellucci was right; she was beautiful.

"My name is Willow Rutherford. I have a proposition for you."

"Si, come in." Emilio motioned towards the café.

"I thought we could take a drive in the park."

Emilio, admiring the car, shrugged. "Why not? It's a nice day." Lloyd was busy shooing the kids away from the paintwork. Emilio exercised his authority by half-raising his hand, at which the kids scrammed. He then followed Willow in to the car.

He turned to Bellucci. "Get in, you come, too." As an afterthought, Emilio asked, "It's okay if my friend comes, too?"

"I want to talk some private business with you."

Emilio didn't care; he wanted his friend to come. "It's okay, he is my private friend."

Nazarena, sensing mischief, had gone into the café and was watching from the café window. She saw Bellucci follow Emilio into the car and sit down opposite the beautiful woman.

The car pulled away and drove into Battersea Park, watched by several of the locals. Bellucci waved at them like a fat potentate from the window of the rich man's car.

Willow allowed the boys to indulge themselves, examining the upholstery and the finer points of luxury travel; finally she got down to business. "Mr Scala, it's a pleasure to meet you. You are such a lucky man."

Emilio looked at her, running a fingertip over the smooth leather of the seat. "Please, Emilio is my name. What can I do for you?"

Willow put her briefcase on her knees. To do this, she had to put her ankles together and point her toes; this move made her calves look very attractive, Emilio noticed.

"Emilio, I think that I can do something for you. What will you get if Grakle falls in the Grand National?"

Emilio looked at the beauty and laughed. "If he falls over, I get nothing. Nothing. But if he wins, I get three hundred and fifty grand." He laughed again at the thought of it.

"Of course, you do know that Grakle fell in last year's race, along with twelve others horse."

Emilio laughed again. "He was practising."

Willow tried to be more serious. "Do you really want to take that chance?"

Emilio knew what was coming, and he didn't like it much. "That's my business."

Willow dismissed the remark and persevered, "Look, I want to give you some insurance."

Emilio lost his patience, remembering the short conversation with Bellucci. 'Fucking Bellucci, why couldn't he mind his own business?' he thought.

"Have you been talking to him?" Emilio indicated his fat friend, who sat looking out of the window, pretending to be unaware of the conversation.

Without changing position or turning his head, the fat man said, "I never say a word. It's a coincidence."

Willow tried to calm the boys down. "I can assure you this conversation is my idea."

Bellucci chipped in; he wanted to really make his point. "Si, it's her idea; it's common sense, you should sell a bit of your ticket."

Emilio shut Bellucci up with a gesture and turned to Willow. "I don't want to sell anything."

Willow caught his eye. "Emilio, I will give you two thousand pounds for three quarters of your ticket. If Grakle falls, you will still be a rich man. If it wins or is placed, you are guaranteed to win a fortune anyway. Frankly, Emilio..." She clicked open the briefcase. "This kind if money is hard to find. What do you say?"

Emilio looked at the thick piles of crisp white five-pound notes; then he looked at Bellucci, who looked away in mock disgust.

"I'm not sure."

Bellucci never changed position; he remained looking out of the window. The words seemed to come from the back of his head. "Two thousand pounds, think of what it can do for you. Pink mirrors and neon lights."

Willow hammered home the point.

"You can't lose. Whatever happens, you win."

Emilio looked uneasy. "I don't know. This is the first big thing I have done in my life. I don't want to  make a big mistake."

Bellucci was by now really fed up with the indecision. He knew in his heart that Emilio should make a deal. On the other hand, he knew his friend well; he was a stubborn bastard. "Give him five grand, he will take that." Bellucci nodded at his friend. "Won't you? You'll take five thousand."

Emilio gave his friend a belligerent look. "What you don't understand is that unlike you, I feel lucky. If I feel lucky, that's a gift from God. I'm a superstitious man."

Emilio fingered the twisted red coral horn that hung around his neck; it lay against his chest under his shirt. Willow watched him. She sensed that he was weakening.

"Okay. Five thousand pounds, that's my final offer." Willow said convincingly.

Emilio twisted his lucky charm as he thought about the offer. "I will take a chance, I no sell. Stop the car; I walk home."

Bellucci wasn't finished. "Aspete, aspete. I will talk to him, give me your telephone number."

Emilio stopped him. "Bellucci. Enough, I don't want to sell, okay? Venga."

Emilio looked at Willow, who had kept her composure during this extraordinary meeting. "Thank you, Miss. It's very nice, but you can keep your money. Venga, Bellucci, venga."

Willow leaned forward and told Lloyd to drive back to the café, her face showing no sign of disappointment. She tried once more, slowly closing the briefcase. It didn't work. Emilio fought the temptation to sneak one last look at the bundles of notes.

At the café, Emilio and Bellucci climbed out of the car. Willow handed Emilio her card, desperate. This was a hard man or a really stupid one. She really needed some small sign of progress; she knew that her offer made sense, but this man was extraordinary.

The sign came as she glimpsed Emilio reading her card. "Wilhelmina, that's a nice name."

Emilio gave Willow his best Italian smile, his blue eyes flashing under his dark eyebrows. She noticed for the first time how handsome he was.

"If you change your mind, telephone me. The Grand National is a hard race to win."

"Hey, life's hard."

Emilio laughed as he closed the car door. Willow wound down the window; she hadn't finished. "Grakle fell last year; you remember that as you make up your mind."

Willow looked hard into Emilio's eyes; he looked back

'God, she is beautiful,' he thought.

"Maybe you hear from me, maybe you don't. It was nice to meet you Wilhelmina, ciao."

Emilio waved and turned to enter the café. Nazarena was at the window; she let the curtain drop.

On the pavement, Emilio had one last thing to say to Bellucci; his mood had changed from a belligerent, hard man to his usual playful self. "Bellucci, it's magic, this thing; if the bloody horse wins, I'll be a magic man, can you imagine? A millionario. I wanna have a look at Grakle. Let's go tomorrow, let's look at Grakle, then I decide." They crossed the pavement.

"Oi, Bellucci. Wilhelmina, she's beautiful, no?"

The fat man pretended to ignore him. "Yeah, and you are fucking crazy."

# CHAPTER TEN

The next morning found Nazarena in a state of confusion. All this sweepstake activity had intruded on her humble but well-ordered life. She had come to understand and manage her life in Battersea, and she knew how to make a small profit from her endeavours in the café. In the summer, the household had a good flow of cash by the ghetto standards; she knew how to hide bits of cash, not in order to deceive her husband, but to feel the confidence and security of a nest egg for her growing family. This made her feel useful and in control, in an alien environment so different from the three-hectare farm in the village Isola di Liri where she had grown up.

She was ten years old when her best friend, Emilio, the handsome eldest son of Antonio and Angelina Scala, had promised someday to marry her. They had fallen in love among the wild herbs and the goat herds on the mountains of Isola. That was before he had run off with the circus that had come to the village one Easter. Before he left, Emilio had promised to make his fortune, and one day send for her.

The letter arrived with a boat ticket and some money a few days after her seventeenth birthday, the year 1920. She packed a small bag with her few possessions and some bread and cheese, and ran away to follow Emilio. She had never left the mountains around the village before; her experience of the outside world was non-existent. The seventeen-year-old peasant girl made the terrifying journey to Genoa. It took three weeks.

She spent three days at the station in Rome, too terrified to get on the train. At the docks in Genoa, she was befriended by another emigrant family in search of a new life. They helped her get on the boat—a liner that had come from South Africa, stopping briefly in

Genoa en route to England.

Emilio had found himself a job at the Slade School of Art, as a model. His dark good looks and the classical proportions of his body put him in great demand with several of the important painters of the day. When he finally met Nazarena at the London docks, he had one hundred and twenty pounds in his pocket and a shared room with a widowed Italian woman, Mrs. Bellucci and her tubby son, Alphonso, who became Emilio's best friend. Emilio married Nazarene, they partitioned the room, and the Scalas set up home.

Since the arrival of the two-thousand pound prize, Nazarena had felt increasingly insecure. The woman with the silk stockings in the big red car—who was she? What did she want from her husband?

Emilio and Bellucci hovered around the kitchen, reading the racing newspapers, dressed in their best clothes. They were going away for the day, and Nazarena didn't know where, and this worried her— particularly because she and her friend Selma were preparing to make a little surprise party for Emilio and his friends to celebrate their good fortune.

Bellucci scanned the racing papers and found what he was looking for: the address of Grakle's trainer, Mr. Tom Caulthwaite.

"Emilio, it says here that Grakle is trained in a place called Hednesford, near Walsall."

Emilio threaded his watch through the buttonholes in his waistcoat. "Good, let's go."

Nazarena kept her fears to herself as she brushed his jacket. He gave her a hug and kissed the kids. "See you tonight. Come on, Bellucci, let's catch the train."

The boys, in their Sunday suits, swaggered out of the yard, leaving behind a concerned Nazarena.

After a long train and bus journey, Emilio and Bellucci found themselves walking through magnificent woodlands that bordered Cannock Chase. For an hour, they walked along a narrow tarmacadam road that seemed to lead nowhere. The weather was sharp and windy. The hedgerows were bare of leaves, except for the evergreens. Bramble tentacles, their dead leaves withered, had long-since been stripped of their berries. A herd of fallow deer crossed the road, remnants of the vast herds once hunted in these forests by the Plantagenets.

"At least it's not raining," said Bellucci, mopping his brow; he hadn't walked this far since he was a kid. Emilio, a fit man, enjoyed the exercise.

At the next crossroads, stood an inn. The swinging sign was decorated with a horseshoe.

"We must be in the right place. Look, a horse shoe. Let's get a beer."

The sharp rat-a-tat-tat of a woodpecker working on a nearby oak echoed through the forest.

"Yeah. Let's get a beer."

Inside the inn, a couple of farm workers were drinking at the scrubbed plank bar, talking to the barman. All three turned to look at the two foreign-looking gentlemen as they entered. Emilio ordered two pints of beer and joined the already-seated Bellucci, who had collapsed at a small table by the window. The barman delivered two frothy pints and put them on the table.

"There's nothing like a drop of Staffordshire ale after a walk like that. That will be one and eight, if you please."

Emilio paid the man.

"Excuse me, is this Hed.. nes.... ford?"

He had difficulty pronouncing the name. The barman helped him. "You mean Hednesford. It's about a mile up the road."

Emilio looked around the room; a small fire glowed in an open hearth. A few old country artefacts hung on the plastered walls.

"We are looking for the race horses," he said, taking a frothy swig from his pint. He wiped his mouth with the back of his hand "That's good."

"Which horses would they be?" inquired the barman.

"Grakle, the Grand National horse."

Bellucci drank half his beer and belched.

"You want Tom Caulthwaite's place—The Castle, he calls it. Flaxley Green, that's near Rudgeley. It's a good four mile."

Bellucci drained his glass at this depressing news. The beer had brought out fresh beads of sweat on Bellucci's forehead skin. He ordered another pint. The barman went back to the bar, which was just out of earshot, and informed the labourers that the two strangers were definitely foreign.

The younger of the two labourers drained his beer. "I think I'll take the bicycle down to Caulthwaite's and tell him that there are foreigners snooping about. He'll give me a shilling or two if they be the nobblers that the papers are talking about. They did say to keep an eye open."

The barman looked over to the two resting travellers. "You do that, Magnus. You do that."

The labourer left, tipping his cap in the foreigner's direction. Once outside the inn, he bicycled furiously down the lane towards Tom Caulthwaite's place at Flaxley Green.

The barmen delivered the second pint to Bellucci, who still looked depressed at the thought of a further four-mile walk. "Wilf, there, will take you to the castle for a pint or two; he has a cart out back."

Even Emilio looked relieved; he got out of his chair and walked to the bar to negotiate. Two pints later, and with a shiny London half crown in his pocket, Wilf brought the log cart around to the front of the inn.

Emilio and Bellucci drained the glasses and climbed aboard. During the conversation that ensued, old Wilf laughed to himself at the thought of young Magnus puffing himself out on his bicycle. 'If he hadn't been so suspicious he too could have drank a few free pints with the man who had drawn Grakle in the sweepstake.'

On the rickety but pleasant journey, Wilf told the boys about Tom Caulthwaite. He was a master at training steeplechasers. He had trained the winner of the Grand National twice—Eremons in 1907 and Jenkinstown in1910. "I was just a lad then; I had a shilling on both of them."

The cart bounced towards the top of Cannock Chase, and a corrugated hut came in to view.

"There it is. That's Mr. Caulthwaite's place."

Emilio looked at the humble building. "I thought you said he lived in a castle."

"Oh, that's his little joke; he spends most of his time in this hut. He just calls it the castle because it was built for the Prince of Wales, to sleep in when he came up here to   school his point-to-pointers."

The cart stopped at the top of the hill, where Magnus's bicycle leaned against the corrugated hut. A flock of sparrows flew off the tarpaper roof as a tough-looking old gentleman opened the door and stepped out on to the heath.

Tom Caulthwaite in a tweed suit, his bandy legs clad in drainpipe trousers, approached the visitors. An old pair of brass binoculars swung from his right shoulder, and a thick grey walrus moustache hung from his top lip like a pair of miniature bull's horns. His old curly brimmed hat had three well-worn dents in it, and a pair of sparkling old eyes twinkled beneath the brim. He held out his hand.

"Tom Caulthwaite. Can I help you gentlemen?"

Magnus hovered at the side of the shed, pretending to watch a lone horse and rider that cantered up the hill some distance away. Wilf had left his carthorse to graze on the sweet grass of the Chase, and had followed Emilio and Bellucci towards the hut.

"Afternoon, Mr. Caulthwaite. These gentlemen have come from London to see you. They've drawn Grakle in the Sweepstake."

The old man's eyes twinkled even more as he took Emilio's hand in a vice-like grip.

"Good heavens. Magnus there thought you were horse thieves, or worse. You must be Mr. Scala. I wondered if we would get a visit from you."

Emilio looked at the old man, who seemed very small standing in the middle of the wide open space of Cannock Chase.

"Hello, Mr. Caulthwaite. We come to see Grakle. I'm glad we find you."

"You've come to the right place, lad."

Caulthwaite took off his binoculars and gave them to Emilio, pointing down the hill to the horse and rider. Emilio looked down the gentle slope into the valley of heather-lands that seemed to sweep into the distant hills of West Shropshire. Some quarter of a mile away, the lone rider schooled his horse over a series of fences.

"Is that him?" Emilio focused his eyes into the brass binoculars. "He jumps like a stag."

"That's him. God willing, he's a National winner, or I'm no judge."

Bellucci wanted to have a look. Emilio gave him the glasses.

"I've retired, you know. I've won the race twice. But Mr. Taylor of Liverpool begged me to have one more go, and I love the horse, so I agreed. I've booked Bob Lyall to ride him. We have only Easter Hero and thirty-two fences to worry about. Now then, lads, would you like a cup of tea or a glass of beer? Let's go in the castle." He chuckled. "This wind's got a chill in it."

Inside the hut, Emilio was thankful for the warmth that emanated from a cast-iron stove; the flue leant precariously against the corrugated wall, then bent out through a hole in the wood slat roof. The place smelt strongly of liniment and other unidentifiable medicinal smells. Bits of harness and other tack hung on a wooden saddle-horse that ran along one wall.

Tom Caulthwaite took a piece of tack from the saddlehorse. "You see that?" He passed the bunch of leather straps to Emilio. "That's my secret weapon. Grakle is a bit of a puller, so I made it myself, and I shall name it after him. A Grakle, I call it. The two straps cross over his nose, and fasten one on top and one below the bit; stops him getting on top of the bit."

Emilio handled the supple leather and looked at it, mystified. He passed it to Bellucci, who smelt it, then agreed that it was a good secret weapon. They talked about this and that until old Tom climbed from the only chair at the sound of a motorcar outside the hut. "That will be Mr. Taylor, the owner. I'm sure he'll be pleased to meet you."

The door opened before Tom could reach it. In walked Mr Cecil R. Taylor, the hugely successful Liverpool cotton broker. He had paid four thousand guineas to the County Kilkenny breeder T.K. Laidlaw for Grakle and was well pleased.

" 'Ello, Tom. How's he behaving then?"

Taylor nodded at the two characters sitting on the camp bed.

" 'Ello, Cecil Taylor's my name, 'ow do you do?" He held out a hand, and Emilio and Bellucci scrambled to their feet from the low bed.

Caulthwaite introduced them. "This is Mr. Emilio Scala. the lucky man who has drawn Grakle in the sweep."

"Delighted to meet you. Grakle's a winner you know. Er, shall we have a look at him?"

Caulthwaite reached for the doorknob. "He's doing very well, Mr. Taylor. Let's have a look, shall we? I told Bobby to bring him up when he saw your motorcar."

The party left the hut to find Bobby Lyall riding Grakle at a walk, up the last two hundred yards of the hill that dominated Cannock Chase.

# CHAPTER ELEVEN

Willow swept through the entrance of number Forty-One Curzon Street. It was a very grand house, beautifully transformed into the offices of Freeman and Enthoven Solicitors. A secretary sat at an antique desk at the foot of a sweeping staircase. She smiled as Willow approached.

"Good morning, Miss Rutherford. He's been expecting you for half an hour."

"Morning, Maud. I know, I'm late."

Willow ran up the stairs past the glossy oil portraits that lined the walls; rounding the bend in the staircase past the huge bay window, she went up one more flight to the first landing, then threw open the double polished doors.

"Justin. Sorry I'm late, darling. I walked through the park."

Justin Freeman was sitting behind a Louis XV desk. Behind him, hanging from the high Georgian ceiling, were pale blue silk drapes that shaded the light glowing through the massive bay window. He was a tall, effeminate man—a dandy— immaculately groomed and tailored. He had a small yellow rose in his buttonhole and wore gold-rimmed half glasses.

"Willow, you are incorrigible. You are thirty-six minutes late. Lunch is probably ruined."

He rose from his desk as Willow reached him; she threw her arms about his neck and kissed his cheek. "Sorry, darling, I really couldn't help it."

Justin un-wound her arms and led her through a door into his private dining room. The table was laid for two, though it could comfortably seat twelve. Justin pulled out a chair for Willow; when she was seated, he went to the other end of the table, passing a wall hung with quality paintings. He took his seat. Justin's butler immediately began serving the meal, which he started by pouring champagne.

"Now, Willow, this had better be good. I had great difficulty rearranging my day so that I could see you."

Willow raised her glass. "Thank you, darling, it's terribly kind of you. I wouldn't have insisted unless it was absolutely imperative. I have a problem that only you can help me with."

Justin sipped his champagne. "The last time you did this to me nearly resulted in having me struck off."

"That was not my fault. How was I to know the man was an impostor?"

Justin forked a piece of smoked salmon from a gold-rimmed plate. "Hope you like the salmon, caught it myself. The less said about the last episode the better. Now then, what's up?"

Willow tasted the salmon. "Delicious. I need a firm of international lawyers."

"Me!" Justin quipped.

"Yes, darling, you."

Willow took a letter from her bag and slid it down the table. It flew across the highly polished oak and rested against Justin's plate. "That is a list of the people who have drawn horses in the Irish Sweepstake.

With your help, I'm buying a share in all their tickets."

She looked up and cracked a cheeky smile. Justin looked up at the crystal chandelier that hung twinkling over the table. He put his fingers together and shook his head in disbelief. "Willow, what am I going to do with you? Can I get something into your tiny brain? I have cancelled two very important meetings with major corporate clients to see you, and now you tell me the reason is to help you with a dubious gambling hustle."

Willow popped the last morsel of smoked salmon into her mouth. "Justin, you have no imagination. This is a beautiful scheme. It's practically fool proof. All I need is a list of foreign lawyers to tie up the contracts. I'll make all the deals on the telephone myself; it's really simple. I just haven't the time to fly around the world getting bits of paper signed. I can pay them well for their services."

She slid a second letter followed by the four bank-wrapped bundles of notes down the table. Justin picked up the letter and looked at the cash as if it were something dirty, a resigned look on his face.

"That's a rough contract that I drew up; simple, isn't it? And that's the cash to make the deals with." She downed more champagne. "Be a darling, Justin, just this once."

By the end of the lunch, Justin had agreed to help, and Willow had agreed to spend the weekend at Greenfields, his Sussex estate.

After her successful lunch, Willow went directly to Grant's office for a progress report.

Lloyd had commandeered the help of a couple of girls from the settling pool; they were handling the international telephone calls. He gave Willow a thumbs-up as she approached him. He was on the phone to Joss Vervelt in Bulawayo.

"Yes, Mr Vervelt. Your horse is forty to one, an outsider. I will guarantee you two thousand pounds for a three-quarter share. I'll have my lawyer visit you tomorrow... Yes, thank you." Lloyd replaced the receiver, looking pleased with himself. He handed Willow the list. "Don't just stand there; earn your money. I've got eight agreements, and I'm seven grand under budget."

Willow looked at the ticked-off names. "Oh, these are the easy ones. Move over; let me show you how this is done!"

Willow struggled with the international operator, having problems with the time differences. She eventually got through to the taxi company that employed Abe Bear as a driver; he wasn't there, but was out celebrating. Two calls later, she connected to the Pussycat Speakeasy in Brooklyn. Abe had drawn Crusader, a horse that was quoted at sixty-six to one.

"Mr. Bear, congratulations, you're a lucky man. I've got a proposition for you."

Two hours later, they took a break to review their progress. Willow and Lloyd climbed the stairs to Grant's office, feeling pretty pleased with themselves. Grant was waiting for them at his desk, and put down what he was doing. "Right," he said, clapping his hands. "How are you getting on?"

Lloyd and Willow sat at the desk and opened their notes. They both said "Well," at the same time. Willow motioned to Lloyd to proceed, which he was pleased to do.

"Well, as of today there are twenty-seven horses left in the race. We have bought six horses; they won't run. Cost five thousand four hundred pounds. Sidi did well. We gave him eight horses to deal with. He did them all except Easter Hero, who had goldfish swimming about in his water bucket—at least, they were swimming about, until Sidi dropped a potion in it. The dead fish gave the game away."

Grant was not impressed with this bit of mismanagement. "You're not taking a load of unnecessary risks putting this together, are you?"

"No, no, Mr.Grant. That was just an unfortunate accident."

Willow took over. "Of the twenty-seven runners left, we've made deals with eighteen of the ticket holders. By tomorrow night, we'll have got to the rest."

Grant thought this was too good to be true. "What, no bad news?"

"We do have a couple of problems." Willow said sheepishly.

"Problems? What problems?" Grant enquired.

"Well, the Italian who's drawn Grakle won't sell, nor will the Irishman who's drawn Easter Hero. He's a very rich man who bought thousands of tickets and thinks his horse can't lose."

"Is that it?" asked Grant.

"No. We can't buy Gregalach's ticket. The owner of the ticket has already made a deal and doesn't want to know." Lloyd had broken this piece of news.

Grant suddenly realised that their plan was in trouble. "You know what happens if one of those three wins, don't you? We lose our money, don't we?"

Willow got up and walked to the window. She looked fabulous bathed in flashing neon light. She turned to Grant. "Are there bigger bookmakers than you in England?"

Grant was annoyed at the change of subject, and didn't much like the question. He was a big bookie, but he wasn't the biggest. "A couple," he eventually said reluctantly.

"Bookies big enough to lay a horse to win three hundred and fifty grand?"

Grant looked at the beautiful Willow. "Are you asking me if I can make a big bet? Well, the answer is yes. I'm Toby Grant, remember?"

"Then everything is okay. We can't lose, and that's why the scheme won't work without you, Toby. Tomorrow we'll try again to buy a share in these tickets; if we can't, and it's final, we must back these three horses with big enough bets to cover all our costs and profits, should one of them win."

Grant was not pleased. "Do you think I'm made of money?"

Willow came back to the desk to calm Grant down. "Wait, let's work this out, George. What are the ante-post prices of Gregalach, Easter Hero, and Grakle?"

George looked at his notes. "Let's see. To win three hundred and fifty grand, at twenty to one, we'll have to stake seventeen and a half grand. The thirty-three to one shot will need a nine grand bet, and twenty-one grand on the hundred to six shot."

"At those prices, it will cost us forty-seven thousand five hundred pounds in bets; add that to our other costs of one hundred and forty grand, that means I'm in this for... one hundred and eighty thousand five hundred pounds."

"I know, Toby, but our guaranteed return, even if one of the backed horses wins, is three hundred and fifty grand. Even if our backed horses are first, second, and third, we make one hundred and seventy grand profit. Any other result and we make more than that."

Willow threw down the challenge to the worrying Grant. "Toby, it's never easy to make this kind of money. That's why I came to you; I know you can handle it. We still have time to buy those tickets, but if we can't, you just have to make those bets. Do you think you can do it?"

Willow had managed to back Grant into a corner; his ego wouldn't let him back down. Besides, he was already committed. "Of course I can do it."

Willow made her first physical move toward Grant, kissing him on the cheek.

"That's great. This is going to work out; we'll have the whole thing tied up well before the race, you'll see."

The meeting broke up when Willow invited Grant to have dinner with her. This latest hiccup had rattled Grant, and Willow felt the need to smooth his feathers.

# CHAPTER TWELVE

Umberto cracked his minstrel's gap-toothed smile at Selma as she passed around the café, pouring Chianti into any empty glass. His old face crinkled into a bony, hollow-faced grin as she filled his glass; being this close to a rosy-cheeked, sweet-smelling virgin was a bit much for him.

Resting his mandolin craftily on his knee, with his now-free hand, he pinched Selma's tit. Her rosy face turned several shades deeper pink as she stood, mortified with embarrassment. She prayed that no one had noticed.

Umberto played a long, trembling chord on his mandolin, the introduction to a well-known Neapolitan dirty song; keeping the chord going until he was quite sure that he had everyone's attention he burst into song.

Mortified, Selma ran to Nazarena for protection. She obliged by putting her arm around the young girl and, at the same time, delivering an appropriate string of insults to the dirty old bastard. This exchange was much appreciated by the company, who cheered Nazarena; but they also cheered the dirty old Umberto. Thus inspired, Umberto's lyrics verged on the obscene.

Nazarena pretended to be embarrassed, but she had grown up with this song since she was a baby. She stirred away at a huge saucepan; in it, nearing perfection, was her special pasta sauce. She dipped a small corner of bread into it and made Selma taste it. Umberto saw this little bit of feeding, and turned his attention towards Nazarena. Still singing, he complained to the gathering about how hungry he was, implying that the reason Emilio and Bellucci had not come to the party was Nazarena's cooking.

He delivered his insults brilliantly, but why shouldn't he? He had been a minstrel for sixty years. Secretly, he could not remember working so hard. He knew that Nazarena was putting on a brave face in front of all her friends, but it was now eleven o'clock, everybody was hungry, and there was still no sign of Emilio.

Umberto downed his wine and went back to work. The opening line of his next song really made the gathering laugh. It was directed at the absent Bellucci. Even Nazarena cracked up, covering her face with her hands.

Finally, Emilio and Bellucci arrived. Umberto was merciless as he insulted the two no-goods who had kept him waiting for his dinner. Emilio, surprised at the welcoming committee, had to endure an Italian version of 'For He's a Jolly Good Fellow' before he could placate Nazarena, who was obviously seeking attention by pulling a stony face as she pushed bundles of pasta in to a cauldron of boiling water.

Joe brought his father the accordion, and the party took off. A stringer from the local newspaper, who had been hanging about all night, finally saw his chance. He knew the Scalas, as he was a regular customer in the café. With a little help from Bellucci, he persuaded Emilio and the family to pose for a photograph. The reporter took these straight to Fleet Street and sold them to the Daily Express. The paper printed a family portrait on its front page: 'Lucky Emilio Celebrates Sweepstake Win.'

# CHAPTER THIRTEEN

Willow sat at Grant's desk, watching him work. She and Lloyd had worked through most of last night and all through the day, tying up the ticket purchases. They now had a share in all the tickets save for Grakle, Gregalach, and Easter Hero. Now it was up to Grant. He was on the phone and under pressure, trying to lay a series of big bets with his peers.

He dialled the number of Jimmy Larkin, a bookmaker in Manchester, the biggest commission agent in the north. "Hello, Jimmy? Toby Grant. How's it going? Are you taking plenty of money on the National?... Good. I've taken too much money on three horses, I'm looking to lay some off. What price for Easter Hero?... Thirty to one! It's thirty-threes everywhere else... Okay, let me have ninety grand to three. Hold on, there's more. Gregalach. What price? Sixteens—now you're really taking liberties. Forty-eight grand to three; yes, I'll take it. Now then, I've got one more. Grakle, what price?"

Jimmy Larkin refused to lay a bet on Grakle. He told Toby the bad news.

"Grakle's been backed to favourite this morning. It was a hundred to six yesterday; now it's ten to one and moving. I'm not laying it 'til it settles down. You must have been slinging a lot of money about. The word is out—you've been trying to lay that bet all day. Sorry, Toby, I can't lay it. Try Sir Rupert."

Toby put down the phone. He gave Willow a cold look. "If one of these horses wins and I'm not on, I'm going to lose a bloody fortune."

Willow pushed him. "I know that. You told me that you could make these bets."

Grant felt bad for a couple of reasons; one, he had got nowhere with Willow at dinner last night. It was a very pleasant dinner, but she had parried his advances expertly. Secondly, he had only managed to get a fraction of the three necessary bets covered; on top of that, the prices were fluctuating as a result of his efforts.

"I can," he said. "It's just not as easy as I thought."

He dialled another number. "Hello, Rupert—Toby! Toby Grant... Not bad. You like to take a nice bet... I want twenty grand to win, Grakle in the National. What odds will you lay me?"

Sir Rupert Osborne, society bookmaker and a very well-informed man, listened to Grant. He had been expecting this call. He didn't like Grant much; he was a bit too clever.

"Afraid not, old boy. Rumour has it that you've got a bit of a shady going. Bought a lot of Sweepstake tickets, haven't you? Let's just say I don't like the smell. I don't know what you're up to, but whatever it is, I don't want it to cost me a lot of money, do I?"

Willow watched Grant's face hopefully.

"That's not like you, Toby, after the business we've done together." Sir Rupert doodled on a pad, enjoying the phone call. "Should have cut a few people in, old chap. We bookmakers should stick together."

Sir Rupert hung up and dialled a number. "David? Rupert. What price for Grakle...? Ten grand to win. Thank you." He replaced the receiver and smiled to himself.

Toby lit a cigarette. "Look, why don't you let me get on with this? You're making me nervous."

Willow stood up. "Okay, Toby, I'll leave you. Please get those bets on. If any of those three get in the frame, we've all been wasting our time."

Toby looked under pressure. "Don't I know it, and on my fucking money." He looked over to George. "Show Willow out, then come back up here. I'm going to need you."

Toby's telephone rang and he picked it up. It was Andrew Hardie, calling from Glasgow. "Toby, I hear you're having trouble getting a bet. Maybe I can help you?"

A relieved Toby explained his problem to the Scottish bookmaker. Hardie, a hard Glaswegian, offered Grant odds of twenty-five to one on Easter Hero, and told him he could put as much as he liked on it. The odds were bad, but Toby took the bet, which meant adding six grand more to his outlay. Andrew Hardie had heard on his grapevine that Easter Hero had been got at and felt he was taking money for old rope. He refused to take a bet on Grakle and Gregalach. Toby felt a little better; it had cost him, but at least now he only had two horses to worry about.

Associates of Justin Freeman were busy on several continents, paying over money and tying up agreements. The bad news was that George Lloyd had been forced to go over budget; however, he had a plan to rectify this situation. After showing Willow out, George came back into the office to sit at his boss's desk. He gave the list of completed transactions to Grant. "Having trouble getting the bets on?"

Grant looked at the list. "Never mind about what I'm doing. What are you doing?"

George looked pleased with himself. "I'm all done, Mr. Grant. I think I can save us some money if you can hold off backing Grakle until you go to the race track."

Grant gave a false laugh. "That's a laugh—hold off. I can't get a penny on the bastard. Now let's do some arithmetic to find out what kind of a mess we're in. Make a note of this; I've backed Easter Hero twice, three grand at thirty to one, and ten grand at twenty-five to one, outlay thirteen grand instead of the projected nine. If it goes in, we draw three hundred and forty grand. Grakle's been backed to favourite, ten to one. I have to get thirty-five grand on it at that price instead of the twenty one that we anticipated. Gregalach is holding its price; so far I've got seven and a half grand on it at twenties. That means I've got to get a further ten grand on, and presuming I can get these last two bets on, we will have laid out sixty-five grand in bets. Add that to the hundred and forty you've spent."

George interrupted his boss and coughed. "I've spent a hundred and sixty! I had to pay more than five grand to two of the punters; they were playing hard to get."

Grant looked at him and was about to vent his frustration, but he took a deep breath instead and decided there was no point; he knew his servant had done his best.

"Right, your hundred and sixty plus the sixty-five, that's two hundred and twenty-five grand I've invested."

George had to interrupt once more. "There are some other costs to add to that total."

Grant smashed his hand down on the desk. "For fuck's sake, what's going on here? I've been wasting my fucking time. We were supposed to make a fat profit out of all this work, and it's disappearing before my eyes. How much more have I done?"

Nervously, George apologised. "Six grand to the lawyers, two grand to Sidi."

"Is that it—two hundred and thirty-one grand, is that it?"

"Yes, Mr. Grant, that's it. We still can't lose; at the very worst, if we're really unlucky, we break even."

Grant was seething. "I don't want luck to have anything to do with this, understand?"

George shuffled his papers, knowing that the only problem that they had was the fact that his boss hadn't got his bets on. "You will get those bets on, and then we're in the clear."

Grant hissed. "If I don't, it will be more than my money that will be lost around here."

George shuffled up his papers and stood up. "Yes, Mr. Grant. Will you be needing me for anything else?"

Grant shook his head. "No, that will be all."

George let himself out and went back to his office, in the settling room. A dozen or so workers were tallying betting slips and counting money. Their chief, a Mr. Crabtree, beckoned him over as soon as he entered.

"George, look at this. We are taking a ton of money from South London, on Grakle. If it wins, we'll get a caning!"

He showed George two wads of betting slips. Lloyd banged the desk for attention. "Listen, everybody, take no more telephone bets on Grakle. Offer five to one that should put them off."

He turned back to Crabtree. "Now, if you will excuse me, I have a lot to do."

Lloyd picked up a telephone and dialled the operator; he asked for a long-distance number, and held on. "Hello, Snowy. Well...? Look, I don't care if you have to start World War III. That horse must not run—now get on with it."

Snowy and Ginger—Grant's two main, hard men he used for everything from collecting debts to denting the heads of defaulting punters—sat in a car parked on the edge of a Cheshire forest, hidden by a bank of laurels that bordered the road from Flaxley Green to Hednesford. Snowy swigged from a hip flask.

"It will be light soon, it's got to pass sooner or later." He screwed the cap back on to the hip flask. "Have I got time for a kip? I'm knackered."

Ginger pulled up his collar and hat brim down; he moved his shoulders into a car seat sleeping position. Ginger passed the flask to his partner. "No, you fucking well haven't. If we fuck this up, we're dead. Have a swig and keep your eyes open."

Snowy snatched the flask back before Ginger could get the top off. "Listen, I think we're in luck."

The two men listened. Snowy wound down the window so that he could hear better. "Yeah, there's a car coming. If it's a horsebox, let it pass and follow it."

A few seconds later, a Ford horse van passed the laurel bushes. Ginger switched on the ignition, pushed the long handle of the gear stick into first, and crept into the lane. The horsebox was already out of sight around a bend in the twisting lane. Picking up speed, Ginger gave chase until he had the horsebox in sight. He settled down and followed the horsebox until both vehicles were on a straight piece of road that ran downhill for a quarter of a mile.

"Do it!" growled Snowy.

Pulling his hat down on his head, Ginger put his foot down, gaining on the horse box that rolled along at a leisurely speed. The Ford came quickly up behind the horsebox. The two men opened their respective doors.

"Give it the boot and jump," Snowy barked the instructions.

Seconds before impact, both men jumped, landing in their respective hedgerows. The Ford careered on, smashing into the back of the horsebox. The box shattered, leaving the bare chasse and the driver's cab to roll forward and jump the verge, where it wedged into the roadside hedge. A goat sprang from the wreckage as the Ford, two wheels up the bank, wobbled and came to rest.

Snowy had landed badly, thumping his hip on a tree stump. Ginger had rolled into the tentacles of an overgrown bramble patch. The driver of the horsebox climbed from his cab, holding his neck. The goat, unhurt, took the opportunity to munch grass on the verge.

Ginger picked himself up and helped the moaning Snowy to his feet. At that moment, a second horsebox came down the hill and stopped at the crash scene. Out of it climbed trainer Tom Coulthwaite. "Are you all right, John?"

John rubbed his neck. "Neck's a bit sore, governor. I'm all right for that. The van's a mess."

Tom Coulthwaite surveyed the scene. "Don't worry about that, John. Sit in my cab while I deal with these villains."

Coulthwaite opened the doors at the back of his horsebox. Two grooms walked down the ramp, and a big race horse swung his head out of the back of the box. Coulthwaite and the grooms walked back up the lane to the two bedraggled villains.

"What the bloody 'eck do you think you're doing? You could've killed someone."

Ginger, supporting Snowy, became indignant. "Our brakes failed."

Old Tom Coulthwaite was furious; his grey moustache twitched. "Your bloody brains failed. I know what you were trying to do; you were spotted hiding in the bushes by a poacher friend of mine. You see that horse?" Coulthwaite pointed to the racehorse that had walked out of the box to join the goat at the verge. "Well, that's Grakle, who I presume you attempted to kill. Well, you've failed; he's going to run in the National, and he's probably going to win."

Snowy rubbed his shoulder. "I don't know what you're talking about. Our brakes failed; we're lucky to be alive. We had to jump from the car—look, my mate has really hurt himself."

Coulthwaite shook his head in disbelief. "You please yourselves; we have work to do. We're going to the races. I can't prove what you did, and frankly I don't care. Our horse is all right, so we will take our leave. I'll be sending a policeman up from the next village to deal with the insurance and wreckage, so you can tell him about your brakes. I shall tell him what I think."

Coulthwaite turned to his two grooms. "Come on, lads, we have a race to run."

Coulthwaite and his grooms loaded Grakle and his friend the goat back into the undamaged horsebox, then drove off. Snowy and Ginger stood in the road, rubbing their wounds.

"We fucked that up pretty good; now how do we get out of this mess?"

"I don't know," replied Ginger, putting his weight against the front of the Ford in an attempt to move it. "Come on, give us a hand; the copper will be here in a minute."

Snowy picked up his hat. "Come on, lift up from the bumper."

# CHAPTER FOURTEEN

Out on the Aintree racecourse at Becher's Brook, Bushy Cooper, chief fence builder for the racecourse, was at work with his team of labourers putting finishing touches to the great fence. Bushy stood on a pile of spruce branches that filled a large cart. The horse in the shafts had jumped this fence when he was an eight-year-old; now, as Bushy worked, the horse was much older than that. Bushy forked another faggot of twigs up onto the top of the fence and climbed up to tuck it into place The breath of the labourers could be seen in frosty puffs in the cold early morning air. Two riders approached, bringing their mounts to the fence to let them smell and look at the great obstacle.

One of the riders shouted up, "Don't make it too hard, Bushy."

Bushy didn't stop in his labours. "It's like a feather bed, Mister, a feather bed."

The riders turned their horses to ride up the course and look at the water jump.

At the café in Battersea, a huge crowd had gathered. Nazarena was already at work, serving early morning tea and sandwiches. The café itself was packed; Selma washed dirty cups and plates. Young Joe spread margarine thinly on slices of bread, making piles of them on a table behind the counter.

Emilio and Bellucci, dressed in suits and new Astrakhan collared overcoats, were prepared for a exciting day at the races. Emilio had hardly slept, lying awake most of the night, thinking. 'Crazy bastard,' he thought. 'Turning down a guaranteed five grand.'

Then another thought took shape: what if he won? How totally incredible life would be for him and his family, and they would be real millionaires, protected for generations from poverty—a thing that he knew only too well. He remembered the first few years after leaving his village, barefoot, following the circus, living on the handouts of the Bandinis, who took pity on the willing and starry-eyed young boy. The circus, more of a travelling family troop if the truth be known, disbanded soon after Mario Bandini broke his neck falling drunk off the top of three rickety chairs while attempting a handstand trick that he had done successfully for forty years.

After that, Emilio drifted to Rome, where he made friends with poverty, the Spanish steps, and the beggar boys vying for position to hustle the tourists. Constantly beaten up by the strongest, if you survived long enough to become strong, you might just earn enough to eat. As he lay awake in bed, he could feel those long gone pains of desperation and hunger.

Five thousand pounds; if that was all he would be left with after the race, it would not be so bad. 'And if the horse wins I take home a hundred grand.' He had contemplated all this, and sleep would not come. What was he doing? There was in reality only one thing to do: take the money and sell part of his ticket. Be happy and content whichever way the dice fell. It was so obvious; why lose sleep? Greed was a terrible thing.

The last thought did it. No, it was not greed that motivated his stubbornness. He knew why he had not sold his ticket. He felt lucky. On that thought, he fell into a sweet sleep.

Emilio gave last-minute instructions to the bespectacled man from the radio shop. "Put the radio up on a shelf where everyone can hear it. Just here above the counter, then we hear it inside and outside."

Satisfied, he left the electrician to wire up the huge Pye wireless.

Bellucci, shaved and dressed in his new overcoat, dried dishes for Selma as she washed up.

"Bellucci, come on, it's time to catch the train."

Nazarena straightened Bellucci's tie and brushed his coat, then did the same for Emilio. Emilio was puzzled by the absence of any of his friends; there was no sign of DeMarco, or Alonzi, or Corsini. In fact, he had not seen any of the boys for days. As they walked across the road to the station, followed by a crowd of locals, Bellucci asked Emilio, "Where are all the boys? You would think they would come to wish you luck."

The train left the station, steaming out into the morning mist. The crowd cheered and waved. Little Jimmy the paperboy ran along the platform to shout, "Good luck, Emilio!" through the carriage window. His cry echoed down the platform. The opaque glass of the station clock glowed like a moon; the black curly hands said seven o'clock.

Willow lay in her deep bath, bubbles bursting under her chin and releasing the scent of Jamaica limes. This was going to be a long day. Six in the morning was not a good time for a young lady to be up and out of her bed. Toby had wanted her to make the trip to Liverpool with him, but she had declined; today she would watch the play unfold in much better company than a flashy little bookmaker. She intended to spend the day as the guest of Lord (Bunkie) St. Ledger in his private box at the top of the new stand at the Aintree Racecourse.

She could hear the rustle of tissue paper; that meant that Monique, her maid, was laying out her clothes. Clever little Monique, she could nurse a girl's wardrobe through a couple of seasons.

The bubbles in the bath had subsided. Willow stood, and picked up a huge Indian ocean sponge that she had allowed to soak up copious amounts of water from the cold tap. She squeezed it against her breasts and shivered as the icy liquid cooled her steam-hot body. Refreshed, she climbed out of the bath into the outstretched huge fluffy towel that Monique held for her.

"Madam must hurry; His Lordship's auto will be here in one hour, and we must do your hair."

With Monique's help, Willow dried herself, slipped on a satin robe trimmed with feathers, and wafted in to her bedroom. She checked the clothes neatly laid out on the satin bedspread that matched the curtains and the padded panels of the wall-length wardrobe. Then she sat at her dressing table to let Monique go to work with hogs hairbrushes and curling tongs.

Willow felt pleased with herself, and why not? Had she not all but climbed out of a huge financial hole? Had she not done what her shrewd father had always taught her? What surprised her was the way she had slipped into the rather dubious aspects of the Sweepstake scam; let's face it, she had stooped to criminal activity, and God, it was exciting, though on reflection she would rather be rich than have to work this hard. Today she would play at being very rich.

Lord St. Ledger's limousine was waiting at the pavement as Willow left her flat, immaculately dressed for a day at the winter races, in an ankle-length cashmere fox collared coat over a two-piece flecked tweed suit. She knew that the fox-fur hat was outrageous.

She immediately recognised the faces of the three beautiful girls that already reclined in the luxury of the sleek car. 'Damn the man, expecting me to travel with his harlots. The swine has invited his entire harem.'

Willow swept past the liveried chauffeur, sinking into her seat as he closed the door.

"Hi, girls, you all look gorgeous." Which they did, and why shouldn't they? They were, after all, the courtesans of England's wealthiest sporting Earl. The girls were driven across a misty Hyde Park, passing a company of mounted Household Cavalry on an early morning ride.

The courtesans were not ladylike in their appraisals of this handsome body of men. Willow amazed herself by falling into the spirit of frivolity expressed by her fellow passengers. 'Wouldn't they just like to know what I have riding on the Grand National?'. She knew there was no point getting snooty; it would only get back to Bunkie. She wouldn't give him the satisfaction. For the time being, she was happy to talk nonsense with these pretty young things.

At Paddington Station, Lord St. Ledger's private Pullman had already been connected to the back end of the Liverpool train. The limousine drove directly to it along the platform, scattering the boisterous first- and second-class travellers, the hucksters, the tipsters, and the Jehovah's Witnesses, who paraded the platform with their placards, hollering Bible quotes of impending doom. The girls transferred to the comfort of the Pullman to join the distinguished guests of His Lordship.

Grant, from experience, had taken his first-class seat early; he sat in a compartment reserved by various London bookmakers, who could always be found on the early train heading for any big race.

The great steam engine let out its final departure whistle, then jerked to get the tremendous weight of a thousand punters moving. After two or three chugs, the huge wheels slowly turned and rolled forward; escaping jets of steam and smoke created the exciting smell of rail travel that lay like a thick carpet on the deserted platform, long after the train had left it.

Grant travelled with his two track men, who would handle the Toby Grant bag in the silver ring. They would pick up a tic-tac man at the course. Grant enjoyed chatting to his fellow bookmakers, none of them his peers. He hoped that during the journey he would be able to lay some of the bet on Grakle, who was still giving him problems. In the meantime, he was happy to chat and contemplate the days when he first hoisted his bookie's bag onto a train to go off to do battle with the punters at a racetrack.

In front of him on the luggage rack were the bags of his fellow bookmakers—fat leather bags with beautifully painted names. Monty Shine from Bermondsey kept his bag at his feet as he sat there on the floral plush, his brown bowler pressing down on his ears. Next to him sat his tally man, Vinnie Vogle, who had worked for Grant in the old days. Rumour had it he could throw his book away and still memorise every bet struck in a day, and the ticket numbers. He was a real soldier of the bookmaking trade.

In the window seat, his bag stuffed into the net of the luggage rack above his head, sat John Stubbs from Hounslow. Grant was waiting for a chance in the conversation to back Grakle with him. Stubbtubss was the only man in this carriage who could stand a loss of forty or fifty grand, but Grant knew that he would have to box clever to get him to take a big bet.

"What's the money been coming for in Hounslow then, Johnny?"

John Stubbs was happy to discuss his business with the powerful Toby grant. "I've taken a pile on Drumstick. The owner lives down our way, and the whisper has driven my punters crazy. You don't want a bit of it, do you?" Specks of spittle shot between the man's protruding front teeth.

"Might do," said Grant, thankful that Johnny Stubbs had opened negotiations. "It's been laid with me to win sixty grand."

Stubbs was pleased to advertise the calibre of his business in this company; he hoped that everyone was listening. Grant had taken a fifteen hundred pound bet on Drumstick earlier in the week, laying sixteen to one.

"I'll back it with you, fifteen hundred quid if the odds are right." John Stubbs would be very happy to take the percentage.

"How's fifteen to one?"

Toby's settler, Billy Doyle, pricked up his ears in case he should be needed.

"To do you a favour, I'll take seventeens."

Stubbs thought for a minute; he'd been bullshitting. The fact was that he had backed Drumstick himself at twenty-five to one weeks ago. He took Grant's offer, which meant he now had a free bet of eight to one on Drumstick.

"You have a bet, my friend." Johnny Stubbs made a note in his little black book. Feeling pleased with himself, he lit a cigar.

"Have you got that, Bobby? Fifteen hundred quid at seventeen to one with Johnny Stubbs on Drumstick."

Grant leant back in his seat; he had just earned a free even-money bet on Drumstick. No big deal, but a percentage was, after all, a percentage. He cast a satisfied glance at the other bookmakers, hoping to give the impression that he might be open to more business, and that his pally, magnanimous gesture might help him when he tried to get a few quid on Grakle.

The bookies discussed the race for the next hour, each presenting his selection. Grant thought he was in luck; in this company, at least, there was not one person who fancied Grakle. The general feeling was that Grakle had been artificially backed to favourite. Grant was relieved; apparently the word had not spread to the lower echelons of the bookmaking fraternity that he was desperate to back Grakle to win three hundred and fifty grand.

"Well, I fancy it." Grant lit a cigarette from a silver case with a built-in lighter, and leaned back in his seat, hoping that the motley gang of bookies would take the bait, or at least some of them.

Johnny Stubbs shifted his tweed-clad frame, his fat top lip permanently parted from the bottom one, revealing the protruding tombstone teeth. "You can back it with me. I'll take as much as you like."

This was what Grant wanted to hear; he tried not to be that interested, preferring to survey the passing scenery than to give Johnny Stubbs an answer.

"I'll take what you like at five to one." A drop of spit flipped from his lower lip to dissolve in the thick tweed of his jacket.

Grant's heart sank. Five to one. He couldn't back it at that price; in his estimation, it was five to one that a horse could finish the race, let alone win it. Grant feigned joviality. "Thanks a lot, Mr. Stubbs. You're in a generous mood." Then under his breath, he cursed, "The wet-lipped, percentage-scraping bastard."

Mousey Taylor, a small thin man in an almost yellow check suit, shifted in his corner seat next to the corridor window. "I'll take two hundred pounds at six to one."

Grant gave the thin man a disdainful look and didn't bother to answer him, preferring to sink into the gloom of his own thoughts. Fundamentally, Grant was stuffed; his only hope was that the price of Grakle would be better on the track. Or that Grakle would lose, or better still, fall like he had last year. He fervently hoped so. This thought cheered him up as the train rattled towards his moment of truth.

Further down the train in a second-class carriage, Emilio and Bellucci had become celebrities. Bellucci had dropped the word to a fellow passenger that his friend had drawn Grakle in the Sweepstake, and the word had spread through the carriage like oil on water.

It now appeared that everyone on the train was involved in the possibility of being associated in a small way with a potential Sweepstake winner. If Grakle won, hundreds of people would, in future days, relate the story of how they travelled to the Grand National in the same coach as the Sweepstake winner; many of them would claim they shook his hand. All this revelry had the effect of swinging even more punters in to the Grakle camp.

This would not help the cause of Toby Grant.

## CHAPTER FIFTEEN

By midday, the scene outside the Scala café was chaotic. Hundreds of local people, mostly unemployed, had crammed into the street outside the café. Many of them had climbed onto the wall of the bottling factory, where they sat like crows in their black jackets and bowler hats. Nazarena had tried to carry on as normal, doing a roaring trade in sandwiches and rolls stuffed with cheese and tomato, and her speciality bologna sausage; by eleven o'clock, she had sold out of everything edible. She was now fretting at the loss of income. Under siege in the café with a few close friends, she nervously watched the growing crowd through the closed windows, as the children enjoyed the madness.

Joe watched the mounted police trying to keep order on the periphery of the crowd. A film crew with a hand-cranked camera mounted on top of a van, cranking away as it filmed a black-and-white record of human curiosity.

The huge Pye radio, tuned to maximum volume, crackled loudly. Occasionally a voice broke into the music with snippets of Grand National information. None but those at the very front could hear a word. Hopefully in an hour's time, there would be a sufficient hush to hear the race.

Bellucci's old mother, clad in black from her shawl to her toes, sat knitting, occasionally firing words of calming wisdom to the fraught Nazarena, and the rosy-cheeked Selma, who sat talking to Father O'Dwyer. O'Dwyer, although a priest, was a betting man, and was thoroughly enjoying the proceedings. He drank his strong black coffee and listened to the young girl, though his thoughts were somewhere else—the church improvements that would be made if Mrs. Scala became the wife of a millionaire. She was already generous beyond her means. He smiled a yellow-toothed smile as she brought him a plate of homemade biscuits.

"I'm so grateful for you coming today, Father. We can all pray for my husband before the race."

What the crowd in the street expected to see was not clear. She bit the knuckle of her forefinger to ease her worry; maybe they'd come to see a miracle. She looked out through the window to see her quiet little street had become a carnival.

Fed up with the waiting, she wrung her hands, wishing that Scippio would get back with the tricycle and the supplies so that she could sell more of her tasty sandwiches and delicious rolls to this hungry, captive crowd.


Emilio and Bellucci had to fight their way onto the charabanc. The passengers of the London train had converged with trains coming in from the north, and the great Lime Street Station echoed to the sound of the huge sporting crowd. Cars and taxis lined up with signs that had passengers' names scrawled on them. A line of charabancs were available to transport those who were not prepared to walk the four miles to the racecourse or board the crowded branch line train to Fazakerley Station on the course itself.

After a short drive, during which Bellucci played 'Find the lady' with a couple of cockneys at the back of the bus, Emilio stepped down onto the soft turf of Aintree Racecourse. The bus had dropped them at Fazakerley Station, just a couple of hundred yards from Becher's Brook. A fresh breeze lifted his unbuttoned overcoat; he stood there, shaken momentarily by a shiver, then buttoned his coat and made sure his new hat was firmly in place. Letting the other passengers push past him, he drank in the scenery.

It could have been a day in May—a blue sky with a few little floating clouds. There were no trees or woods on the Aintree Racecourse; he could see across the track to Aintree Village and the steeple of Kirby church. To his right, he could see the small stand at the canal turn. This was not the prettiest of courses; in the far distance, he could see the horizon bristling with tall slender Lancashire smoke stacks. Emilio wondered who lived in all the squat little brick houses.

He had never seen a crowd like this. It was amazing, an incredible number of people. There were hundreds of thousands of them. He turned to look down along the full length of the course, following the bright white fence to the enormous wooden grand stand, packed with people. They were even crammed like tiny ants onto the vast sloping roof, beneath which he could see the rows of private boxes that seemed to hang over the steep steps of the punters' stands. Emilio noticed the sold-out sign go up on the race card booth; even the organisers were not prepared for a crowd this size.

"That's where I would like to watch the race." He wondered how much it would cost.

A puffing Bellucci finally climbed out of the bus, swearing. "Bastards. I lose five bob on the find the lady. I put my finger on the queen, and held it there, and the bastard, still he manage to change it."

Emilio laughed; he had lived with the circus, and knew all about the tricky fingers of flim flam men.

The mumbling Bellucci's appearance had not really been enhanced by the addition of a new overcoat and hat. He had shaved this morning but you wouldn't know it, dark patches of blue bristle seeming to cling to the creases in his fat face. They strolled along the cindered track, past marquees of every description, crossing the Melling Road towards the main stands.

"I feel like a million dollars—less, of course, the five shillings I lose to those bastards."

He took Emilio's arm and guided him over to a crowd of people that had gathered around some kind of African witch doctor. The character at the centre of this racecourse vignette was a very tall, very black man; on his head and waving gently in the breeze was a sort of ostrich-feather crown. In one hand, he carried a Rhino tail whip, and in the other, a copy of the sporting life. He wore a multi-coloured robe of thick Nigerian cotton. Peeping from the folds and planted firmly on the turf were the toes of a pair of very expensive handmade shoes.

"I got a horse, I got a horse, I got a horse!" the man cried, to the enjoyment of the crowd. Periodically he smacked the newspaper with the Rhino whip, to punctuate his huckster's dialogue. "You will drink champagne today if you listen to me. I got a horse!"

A fascinated Bellucci dragged Emilio over to the spectacle. He noticed that people were slipping the black man money; in return, he appeared to slip them a piece of paper.

"For half a crown, you can share with me the only certainty of the day—would I lie?"

The crowd responded with a universal voice: "No!"

"You all know me?"

"Yes!" the crowd shouted back.

All this was too much for the gullible fat man. He parted with his two and six and duly received his piece of paper. Emilio, whose mind was on other more important dreams, vaguely watched his fat friend unwrap the witch doctor's folded message. On it was written the word fantasy. Emilio craned his neck to read the message—not that he was that interested, but on the other hand, he had been looking for an omen since he had opened his eyes this morning.

"Fantasy. Fantasia. That's a very good word for a day like this," Bellucci agreed. Screwing up the paper, he threw it away. A little fellow in a thin coat scooped it up. Bellucci guided Emilio into a tent that smelled of food.

## CHAPTER SIXTEEN

Scippio whistled through his perfect teeth as he collected and paid for the list of supplies that Signora Scala had given him, stowing them neatly in the empty box of Emilio's ice cream tricycle. Everywhere he went, they were talking about his boss. 'One day I'm gonna be a big man like Signor Scala.'

Today he was practising. His heart pounded in his shirt, but not from the exertion of riding the tricycle; he was suffering from his first taste of gambler's terror. He whistled to pretend that he was not scared. This morning, he had taken five shillings from his meagre savings and given it to Jimmy the newspaper boy to put on Grakle to win the Grand National. He had never made a bet before, and if this was what gambling was like, he was not sure that he would do it again.

Feeling the butterflies in his stomach, he started to whistle again. He peddled down Battersea Park Road and turned the corner by the South London Bottling Factory to find the café besieged. The crowd had grown threefold; it was now enormous, and there was no way that he could get his cargo through. Being a bright boy, he persuaded Mr. Jenkins, the manager of the factory, to look after Emilio's bike while he ran the gauntlet of the crowd with loafs of bread and other supplies up his shirt.

Nazarena went immediately to work, sliding open the café window to serve the curious and the hungry. She felt better now that she had something to do; all that waiting was a nightmare. Thank God for Father O'Dwyer, and Selma, and Scippio.

She made a sign of the cross and got on with the business of selling three-penny sandwiches.

The music on the radio stopped. A voice began to read out the names of horses and jockeys in the big race. An instant hush overcame the vast crowd.

"Number twelve, Dervish, ridden by J. Tracy."

"Number thirteen, Sox, ridden by B. Candy

"Number fourteen, Grack—" At the mention of the local hero, the crowd erupted into a deafening cheer.

## CHAPTER SEVENTEEN

While Emilio and Bellucci ate pork pies in a striped canvas beer tent, shoulder to shoulder with the hard-core racing folk, Lord St. Ledger hosted a very different kind of meal in a private dining room adjoining his box at the top of the main stand. He tucked into a brace of snipe, their beaks stuffed neatly up their back sides as they lay perfectly baked on inch-thick slices of hot buttered toast; a steaming glazed sauce dripped from their plump little breasts.

St. Ledger took a fair sip from a crystal glass of a rare white wine that had travelled down from his estate in Derbyshire, in hampers together with silver, linen, and the necessary food for a racing luncheon. He watched his dozen or so animated guests pick at the food with some satisfaction. The girls at the table were all, without exception, very beautiful. In the recent past, all had visited his bed— that is, with the exception of Wilhelmina Rutherford; he had not quite got the hang of her. This annoyed him, as she was by far the most beautiful woman at the table. Trouble was, she was too dammed bright. Seemed to lead her own life. Didn't fall for the usual baits. Bloody annoying of her, paying her own expenses in Monte Carlo last year. There was nothing more annoying than an independent woman, particularly when one was so much in love with her.

He carved a slice of snipe breast and popped it under his rather royal-looking moustache. One of his servants poured more wine. St. Ledger eyed his butler, who immediately hovered at his side, bending down to within earshot in order to receive instructions.

"Bartlett, would you fetch the bookmaker?" Then with a raised voice,

"I believe our guests are ready to bet on the second race."

Bartlett nodded and slipped from the box to a more crowded one next door.

"Has anyone found the winner of the next race?" St. Ledger asked his guests

There was much chatter at the table and passing of race cards. Miles Grenfell had a tip from Prince Monalulu, the black tipster. He persuaded the pretty Minnie Barton to have twenty guineas on it. Sir John Mainwaring had dropped a couple of hundred on the first race, and fancied the selection of the Sporting Life's tipster, Augur.

Toby Grant showed no sign of his preoccupation as he entered the box, cheeks glowing as a result of several stiff scotches. Jauntily he approached the table. "At your service, my Lord. I hope you have better luck on this race. What may I do for you?"

Toby Grant produced his little red book, which was quite famous among serious punters. He hovered, pen at the ready. St. Ledger lost concentration for a moment as he caught sight of Greville Hanson getting on much too well with Willow halfway down the table. "Willow, are you going to make a bet?"

"Oh, sorry, Bunkie; The Digger, fifty guineas each way."

Toby disguised his surprise at seeing Willow, and made a note; he made the rounds of the table, returning to his Lordship, where he expected and took a substantial bet on a horse of little talent. As the roast beef was served, Toby Grant took his leave.

Willow was well aware of the crush St. Ledger had on her; she had worked on it for over a year, wanting to turn it into a passion, and for her part she felt she was achieving this but knew that there was more work to do. She flirted lightly with Greville, knowing full well the effect this would have on her host. There would be plenty of time to make amends after the big race. If all went well, she would be twenty-odd thousand pounds the richer, a substantial sum for a young lady to play with; and if anything should go wrong, His Lordship was definitely her next quarry. She had read nothing from Toby's face as he had taken the bets. After this race, she would go to the betting ring to find him.

Emilio was glad he hadn't bet on the first two races; he was far too nervous to concentrate on little matters. If the truth were known, he was a wreck. As the moment of truth rapidly approached, he was having second thoughts as to the wisdom of his stubborn refusal to hedge part of his ticket. He had visions of sitting on that train, listening to Bellucci's curses, and his own for that matter. It would have been so easy to walk in to the café with the extra few grand and plonk it on the table, so easy to watch Nazarena's pretty face light up at her husband's shrewdness at having won, even though his horse had lost. He felt sick and giddy, leaning against the rail to recover. The ominous thought crossed his mind, 'It's too late now.' The race would be off in twenty minutes; even if he did change his mind, it was too late.

The runners were in the paddock having their blankets taken off. Bellucci interrupted him from his thoughts. "Emilio, there is Mr. Coulthwaite—look, it's him."

In the paddock, Tom Coulthwaite was talking to Bobby Lyall, who was dressed in the orange and black colours of Mr. Cecil Taylor, who stood next to the big dark bay horse that had two crisscrossed straps across its face where other horses would have a nose band.

"Let's wave at him. He might let us go in there with the big shots."

Emilio gave Bellucci a doubtful look. He still felt giddy; the blood had drained from his face. He focused on the big horse as it swung its quarters around in a semi-circle, revealing a bank of defined muscle under its polished coat. Restless, Grakle turned again, this time giving a profile of his head and neck. The mane had been braided into seven tight bunches, evenly spaced from the ears to the shoulder. The top half of Grakle's tail had been tightly plaited; the once-flowing horsehair had been braided into a knot that would have done a master boy scout proud. The only colour on the horse was the pale canvas boots on his forelegs.

Emilio looked at the other horses and their jockeys, amid a sea of multi-coloured silks and steaming horse breath. He saw Tom Coulthwaite pull a maroon and royal blue blanket from Grakle's back. The horse was beautiful and very fit, there was no doubt about that, but so were most of the others.

Next to Grakle was Gregalach. Its owner, Mrs. Gemmel, was in deep discussion with Everett, the little jockey who had come from being a midshipman in the navy to winning the race on this horse two years before. Everett stroked the cricket-ball-sized white spot on Gregalach's forehead.

Ten yards away, Easter Hero's long white face looked around him, while his Irish jockey, Johnny Maloney, thought his own thoughts. He had partnered Easter Hero into second place two years before and wanted the win badly. Another Irishman looked over to Johnny Maloney and waved his whip in salute; he'd won the race last year on Saint Golin and was to partner him again. He secretly prayed to the saints for the miracle of two wins in a row.

Bellucci suddenly noticed that his friend didn't look to be enjoying the proceedings. "What's a matter with you? You look like you see a ghost. You no change your mind, have you?"

Emilio rubbed his knuckles, remaining silent with indecision. He was surrounded by thousands of people, yet he felt utterly alone.

"Hey, Paesane, you change your mind, don't you?"

"I just have second thoughts. It's too late now, anyway."

Bellucci grabbed Emilio's arm.

"Come on, let's go, the big bookmaker's over there. Grakle is favourite, and you get a good price. Come on, Paesane."

Grant had been running up and down the silver ring, trying to get money on Grakle. So far his efforts had backed it to win forty grand—three hundred and ten short of his target. He knew he was running out of time. The crowd around him had grown oppressive. He should be enjoying this day; he should be the mastermind behind a massive coup. Instead, he felt like a half-assed punter begging lesser bookmakers than himself to take bets from him. The whole thing stank. Every Bookie on the line now knew he was desperate to back Grakle. The price had settled down at seven to one. Grant walked back to his stand, where his boys were taking money and stuffing it into the bag decorated with the name, TOBY GRANT, PICCADILLY. Toby reverted to the bookie he was and climbed onto the soapbox to practice what he did best: shouting the odds to punters at the races.

"How are we getting on, Toby?" He looked down to see Willow smiling hopefully. "Have you got it all on?"

At the other end of the line, Bellucci approached the bookmaker with a double bag and a big hand-painted nameplate, RORY DUGGAN. The bookmaker was dressed in plus-fours and matching tweed jacket. Standing on a soapbox, banging an ivory-handled cane on his board, he shouted out the odds.

"Yes, sir," he called at the approaching Bellucci, "Ten to one the field bar one."

"Mister, can I have a word with you?" Bellucci shouted above the din.

The friendly Bookmaker bent down and put his ear to Bellucci's mouth. "We have drawn a horse in the Irish Sweepstake, and we wanna sell a share in it."

Emilio, full of misgivings, watched from a distance. He saw the bookmaker hop off his soap box to talk to Bellucci. He felt his heart thumping through his waist coat as he watched and waited. After what seemed an age, Bellucci looked for him; jerking his fat head, he beckoned Emilio over.

"Mr. Scala, you're a lucky so and so; I've read all about you. So you want to sell a bit of your Grakle ticket? I might have just the man for you. Will there be something in this for me if I find you a punter? Shall we say ten percent of what we get if I can make a deal?"

Bellucci shrugged hopefully at Emilio. Emilio shuffled his feet, looked at the bookmaker, and said, "I want twenty grand for half the ticket."

Emilio had worked out the odds; after all, he hadn't had much else to think about for weeks. Half the ticket would get fifty grand if it was third. Seventy five if it was second, or a hundred and seventy five if it won.

The bookmaker did some mental arithmetic. "That's better odds than the seven to one on the board. Ten percent of what I get for you, and I'll see what I can do."

Emilio nodded. The bookmaker told his assistant to take over, whispered, "Wait here," to Emilio, and vanished into the crowd.

Bellucci tried to keep Emilio's mind off the negative aspects of the latest developments. "You'll see, it's gonna be all right."

Emilio rubbed his knuckles as he waited. All around him was the manic fervour of punters at the greatest horse race in the world. Money was changing hand furiously. The voices of a hundred bookies shouted out odds in time to the jerking St. Vitas dance of a hundred tic-tac men, and the crackling echo of the loudspeaker system announced, "In the paddock, the jockeys are beginning to mount their horses." The atmosphere was electric.

Through the crush pushed the red-cheeked bookmaker. He had in tow Toby Grant, who in turn was followed by a tall, beautiful woman. "This is the fellow, Mr. Grant."

Emilio looked past Grant at the elegant figure of Willow. "Hello, Emilio."

Emilio pulled himself together. Jesus, she was beautiful. He took her outstretched hand. "Hello, Willow, we meet again. How are you?"

Willow smiled warmly. She turned to Grant and whispered. "Let me handle this; I know him, he's a funny fellow."

She swung her head, turning her face towards Emilio's to begin her negotiation.

"Excuse me, Willow, can I have a quick word with you?" Grant put his arm around her and took her aside. "Look, he's asking twenty grand for half; offer him fifteen for two thirds. That's my limit. This guy has given me enough aggravation already. Okay? Fifteen for two thirds."

Willow looked exasperated. "Don't say I didn't warn you. This is a hard man. You do it."

Grant stepped forward. "Mr. Scala, in ten minutes, this race will be off, and if your horse falls over, you'll be wiped out." He took a chequebook from his pocket. "Here is fifteen grand for two thirds of your ticket; that's clear profit for you. If the ticket wins, I'll pay you the rest of your winnings after the race. You won't even have to wait for the prize giving."

Emilio, as if pumped up by the presence of Willow, stood firm. "Twenty for half." He gave Grant his best poker face.

"Look, the horses are going down. I'd make up your mind if I were you."

Emilio looked at Willow, who was trying to show no emotion. "I have made up my mind. Twenty for half—take it or leave it."

Bellucci cringed; he turned away holding his breath.

Grant looked at his watch, then at the track. He saw the last of the runners leave the paddock and join the other coloured-silk dots that strung out in a line all the way down to the start.

"Okay. I'll tell you what Ill do. This is my last offer. Twenty for two thirds. That's final."

Bellucci breathed again. He knew his friend was a good poker player, but he had never seen him this good. Grant was waiting confidently, with pen poised.

Emilio suddenly felt relaxed. The crowd came into focus, and so did the whole scene: the grovelling bookmaker, deep lines of desperation at the corners of his mouth. Willow the beauty, standing there with as good a poker face as his. He couldn't read her at all. What was in this for her? Bellucci, standing there, praying for him to take the money.

All the while, thousands of neck-straining connoisseurs, oblivious to everything save for the last-minute scrutiny of the passing steeplechasers.

"Sorry, Mr. Grant, no deal. Willow, enjoy the race. Bellucci, andiamo."

Grant looked once more at his watch. Willow gave him a look that said, 'I told you so.'

Emilio turned his back and made to walk away into the now-frantic crowd.

"Just a minute. Okay. Twenty grand for half your ticket."

Grant borrowed the bewildered bookmaker's shoulder to write as Emilio carried on walking. Grant and the bookmaker went after him. "Listen, I said okay. Twenty grand, all right."

Emilio stopped and turned. He ignored Grant, looking directly at Willow. "I'm sorry, Bella, I changed my mind. He was mucking me about. Come, Bellucci, let's watch the race."

"Madonna. Seite pazzo!, you're crazy!" Bellucci's face had taken on a look of disbelief as had Grant's, not to mention the bookmaker who in all his years had never seen anything like this. He would never forget the lunatics he had met minutes before the start of the 1931 Grand National.

Emilio once again turned to walk away. Grant's raised voice stopped him. "Twenty-five grand for half your ticket."

Bellucci heard the offer and grabbed Emilio's shoulder. "Paesane, listen. Listen to him, take the money."

"I told you to let me handle it. We've lost him; you've jinxed it,

Toby." She walked forward, pushed past Bellucci, and put her hand on Emilio's shoulder. All around them, frenzied faces—flushed with excitement and oblivious of this play within a play—went about their business.

Emilio stopped. He knew it was Willow's hand on his shoulder. He turned, and there she was, inches from his face and still moving closer, until her lips were on his cheek. "Good luck," she whispered as she turned and walked away.

Grant followed her for a few paces. "What was that all about?"

Willow gave him a scornful look that told him he had blown it. "He might win. See you later, Toby."

She pushed her way through the crowd until she could flash her badge and pass into the more civilised area of the racecourse. Leaving the thunderous noise behind her, she climbed the wooden stairs towards the luxury of Lord St. Ledger's box.

Bellucci fought his way through the crowd. He had almost lost Emilio because he had stopped to put a pound each way on Fantasy at two hundred to one. The wake that Emilio made wasn't wide enough to accommodate the fat man; he shoved his bulk through the crush, until they reached the bottom steps of the stands.

"How many times have I got to tell you, you are the most crazy bastard I have ever known?" Bellucci was puffing and blowing, partly because of the push through the crowd and partly because of the fury he felt towards his idiotic friend. "What did she say to you?"

Emilio reached inside his shirt, just below his top button, and pulled out the little red horn, his charm. "She said good luck, that's all; good luck." Emilio gave his fat friend a firm but friendly couple of quick slaps as if to wake him up. "Bellucci, I feel lucky. Whatever happens, we won't forget today."

Major Bracknell climbed the wooden steps of the starter's ladder. Above his head, billowing in the breeze, were the six starting tapes; he signalled to have them pulled down. The groundsmen pulled the levers at each side of the track, and the major watched them stop three feet from the dark green turf. Gripping the rolled up white flag in his hand, he looked at his watch. Behind him, thousands of expectant punters appeared to hold their breath, waiting on him. He imagined for a moment that he was back in the trenches on the Somme, about to signal his men over the hill.

The twenty-eight jockeys milling about on strong chasing horses brought him back. They were not the enemy; they were an august body of brave sporting men, who were about to compete in one of the hardest sporting events ever conceived. It was up to him to give them a fair start, and by God, that was what he would do. "Come on jockeys, bring 'em in."

Quite suddenly a ragged line of riders formed across the track. Several horses spun around. Great Span bucked and almost dislodged its jockey.

"You there, bring him up." The jockey cheekily saluted the Major and did what he was told.

Major Bracknell raised the white flag.

# CHAPTER EIGHTEEN

On the street outside the café, a hush fell, until you could hear a pin drop. It was eerie, considering there were close to a thousand people crammed onto the pavements and road under the railway bridge.

The voice on the radio came through loud and clear. "They're off."

The springs of the starting tapes shuddered and contracted with a clank as the white tapes flew skywards.

For the briefest moment, a listener could hear the birds singing, then the great roar of the crowd swelled up as one hundred and twelve ironclad hooves pounded out on to the hallowed turf of the Aintree Racecourse. The mighty roar of the crowd pumped the adrenalin of the horses and riders alike.

The Grand National was in progress.

The first fence looked an inch high from the starting tapes; it grew with each stride until it loomed up in front of the leading horse. Drin put in an extra stride and leapt in to the sky. What took a moment felt like a lifetime to little T.J. Buckley from County Kildare. In what seemed like slow motion, he was carried into the air, lifting himself out of the saddle to help his Pegasus fly. He would remember nothing more of the Grand National. The field rushed over his small, curled-up frame, the silver stars on the purple silk shirt now mud-splattered; he jerked twice—once from a kick to the thigh, and again from a stamp between the shoulder blades. "Who won?" he asked the nurse when he came-to, three days later.

Bellucci was at the biggest disadvantage; even on his tiptoes, he barely reached five foot six; Emilio fared marginally better by a couple of inches. Trapped as they were in a sea of humanity, they could see little and had to rely on the inaccuracies of the shouted comments of their immediate neighbours. As the colourful charge took Becher's Brook for the first time, Emilio could stand the uncertainty no longer. With the help of his fat friend, Emilio excavated his way to the top of the stands, stopping occasionally to listen for clues as the field took another fence.

As the leaders took the chair for the first time, Emilio and Bellucci found themselves balancing on a wooden shelf directly under the private boxes. Next to them, a serious man of the brogue was giving a spirited commentary. Field glasses glued to his all-seeing eyes, the Irishman read the race; he was good. "Swift Roland went at the water jump—he won't get up from that."

He was right. Dead where he fell, the remainder of the field ploughed over him. Big Black Boy went at the seventeenth, bringing down Sir Lindsey. As the leaders approached Becher's Brook for the second time, Gregalach went to the front and took the huge fence as though it was a kerbstone; Ballasport and Easter Hero jumped it together, followed by the only grey in the race, Glangisia. And then, according to the Irishman, Grakle took fence twenty-three in abominable fashion and placed eighth in the remaining field of fifteen horses.

Emilio didn't care; Grakle had survived the bad jump and had been mentioned at last. This news caused both him and Bellucci to scream with hope. In the stands, Grant's eyes pressed to his glasses. As he saw Grakle make the bad jump, he punched the air in a most unsporting fashion. "Good, that's him stuffed; he'll never win jumping like that."

Back on the shelf, Emilio had his eyes firmly locked on the orange and black shirt that was steadily closing on the leaders. They took the fence at the canal turn, swinging sharp left towards Valentine's Brook.

The Irishman's voice had now adopted a lilting monotonous tone. He was now familiar with all the remaining colours. "Gregalach takes Valentine's by a length and a half from Easter Hero, May King comes next a length away. Then there's a gap of three length to the grey Glangesia racing on the inside of Grakle; further back by a length runs Drumstick, who is about to be overtaken by the fast improving Fantasy. They are all over Valentine's safely, including the loose horses as they gallop away past the Sefton stand towards fence number twentysix."

Bobby Lyall had recovered from his terrifying experience at the twenty third; Grakle had put in an extra stride and crashed down onto the dishevelled spruce branches, causing him to lose his left iron. Thankfully, he had got it back in time for the canal turn and was now in control. He could see Gregalach out in front, jumping like a cat. Easter Hero was up with him; at the next fence, wheeling on, May King landed in third. Bobby Lyle turned his head to grab a quick look behind and caught sight of the scarlet and black colours of Fantasy closing on him. They took fence twenty-eight together. Grakle flew the fence, making Bobby feel the adrenalin pump even harder. Passing Anchor Bridge, where the Melling road crossed the track, Bobby disobeyed Tom Coulthwaite's orders and gave Grakle a crack of the whip. He felt Grakle respond under him.

Emilio and Bellucci jumped up and down on the shelf. Grakle would get a place. As the horses approached the second last, a groan came from the mouth of the Irish man.

"That's me gone—May King's gone, he'd have won it. That leaves Gregalach in front by a length from Easter Hero, with Grakle a length and a half away third. Fantasy is still there in fourth, and the rest of the field are out for a canter."

Emilio could stand no more. He lowered himself down to sit on the shelf; putting his hands to his face, he tried to concentrate on the Irishman's voice, leaving a screaming Bellucci aloft shouting, "Come on, Fantasy! Come on, Fantasy!"

This only added to Emilio's confusion, he being unaware of his fat friend's pound-each-way bet on the black man's tip.

The Irish voice continued the commentary. "They approach the last; Gregalach and Easter Hero will take it together; they're stride for stride. Grakle closes in third with Fantasy a length and a half behind in fourth. He's gone, he's gone—Easter Hero has gone at the last! Grakle goes into second, avoiding the fallen horse. Fantasy makes a great jump. We have a race on our hands here, lads."

Johnny Maloney had a feeling of deja vu as he rode Gregalach out. It was the giant brick cooling tower on his right that reminded him of the sweat and the glory of last year's win. 'Sweet Jesus, will this be one for me Mam, at home.'

He gave Gregalach a smack as he took the gentle left-hand dogleg into the strait. He could feel rather than hear the pounding hoofs behind him; he gave Gregalach another smack to keep him straight and ignored the searing pain in his legs. Crouching as low as he could, he pushed his fabulous horse into the last five hundred yards. Into his vision on his left side, the orange and silver colours of Bobby Lyall slowly took shape. The big dark bay head of Grakle came alongside, nostrils flared, eyes on fire.

"Feck ya Bobby, I'll beat you yet!" Maloney cried as he gave Gregalach a thwack.

Bobby Lyall's lungs hurt too much to answer the Irishman. He struggled to obey Tom Caulthwaite's orders: "Don't use the whip." With two hundred yards to go, a good smack now would win or lose the race. The incredible roar coming from hundreds of thousands of throats seemed like a dream sound; it had an unreal quality about it, but it did nothing to swamp the steady smack, smack, smack of Johnny Maloney's whip.

With fifty yards to go, Gregalach was a head in front. Bobby Lyall whacked Grakle once, then threw himself with a miracle of balance along Grakle's neck. Two strides later, the red and white circle flashed by. Bobby knew he'd won by a neck. He heard Maloney curse before the wave of voices hit him like thunder, and he didn't care that his lungs hurt, or that his legs were shaking uncontrollably, as he stood up in the saddle to ease his champion down.

Emilio, in that calm state that lives somewhere between sheer terror and absolute joy, spoke to Bellucci.

"What happened?" A bewildered Bellucci looked to the Irishman for the answer.

"Grakle won it, a great race. It's Grakle's race."

Bellucci did a very high leap for a fat man, followed by a couple of dance turns; with his arms raised, he gripped Emilio in a bear hug and spun him until they both dropped. The crowd in the immediate vicinity realised that something extraordinary had just happened and caught the euphoria like a highly contagious virus.

"We win. We win the Sweepstake! We win the Sweepstake!" Bellucci and Emilio sang as they danced in each other's arms.

Watching their antics from the balcony of his private box was Lord St. Ledger. Next to him stood Willow and Sir John Bingham. Willow looked down at the teeming mass of people that started fifteen feet below her, spreading out like a thick pile carpet down the sloping steps of the stands and out into the enclosure, stopping in an abrupt, sharp line at the rails of the racecourse itself, where a thick band of emerald green turf cut the crowd in two. On the far side of the green slash, the crowd continued and spread like a dark colourful stain until it was cut again by the ornate fret-sawed wooden gutter of the stands.

In the midst of this multitude, a small knot of people stood out like butterflies in a swarm of ants. It was the animated figures of Emilio and Bellucci.

St.Ledger focused his field glasses on the spot for a closer inspection "What do you suppose is happening there"

Willow smiled as he watched the dancing Italians. "That, Bunkie, is the luckiest man in the world. He's just won the Sweepstake."

Lord St. Ledger pulled down his glasses, realising that they were close enough to see quite clearly without them. "Mmm. The luckiest man in the world, eh? I should like to meet him."

"I think I can arrange that, Bunkie, I know him."

St. Ledger gave Willow a quizzical look. "Willow, you never cease to amaze me—you know the most extraordinary people. Do you think you could get him up here for a drink?"

Outside the café in Battersea, mounted police were keeping the huge chanting crowd in order. Inside, Nazarena lay unconscious on the floor, her head cradled in Selma's arms. Father O'Dwyer fanned her with his handkerchief.

Bellucci's black-robed mother calmly brought over a small bottle of smelling salts and a glass of brandy. "Here, Father, hold this. Take a swig if you like." She cackled. Bending down, she waved the small bottle under Nazarena's nose until her eyes flickered. "There, she'll be all right now. Give a sip of brandy."

Father O'Dwyer put the glass to Nazarena's lips. Her eyes flickered open; she saw the priest and struggled to make the sign of the cross.

"There, there, Mrs. Scala, drink some of this." His nicotine-stained fingers tilted the glass.

Nazarena sipped, coughed, then spluttered the brandy, which ran down her chin as she tried to speak. "Father, did he win?"

"Yes, Mrs. Scala, Grakle won."

Nazarena struggled to make another sign of the cross and whispered, "Jesu Christo."

Bellucci's mother bent to wipe Nazarena's mouth with the small lace handkerchief that lived permanently up her black calico sleeve.

"Father, is it a sin to win so much money?"

The priest chuckled, showing his yellow teeth. "No, Mrs. Scala, it is not a sin as long as you remember that charity is one of God's greatest gifts."

Nazarena closed her eyes; her face took on a peaceful look as she thought about her husband's dream of a cafeteria of pink mirrors and neon lights.

Bartlett struggled bravely through the crowd at the top of the stand. He would rather perform this sort of job himself than delegate it; besides, he wanted to meet the man who had won the Sweep. It wasn't too far from the private box steps to the top of the public stand. Rather than pushing and shoving like a yob, he talked his way through. "Excuse me, excuse me. . ." He was polite but firm, and the approach paid off. He soon found himself in the middle of a ring of dancing lunatics.

"Mr Scala is the one on the fat man's shoulders," Miss Rutherford had told him.

Bartlett tapped Emilio on the knee that hung from Bellucci's shoulder, which had little effect. Bartlett tried again a little harder. Emilio came out of his dazed euphoria to focus on the man in a morning suit. The man was pointing a finger skywards, as the noise was too great to attempt speaking. Emilio agreed with the man and put his hands together as if in prayer and looked up to thank God, as he though he had just been instructed.

Instead of God, above him was Willow, leaning on the balcony with a glass in one hand and beckoning him up with the other. Emilio raised his hat and smiled the confident smile of a man who has just conquered the world. Bartlett watched the communication until he was satisfied that Emilio had accepted the invitation. Taking Bellucci firmly by the shoulder, Bartlett attempted to guide the blind fat man, as Bellucci's hat had been jammed firmly down over his eyes.

Emilio climbed down from Bellucci's shoulders. "Come on, we go to have a drink with the big shots. Look, Willow invite us."

Bellucci looked up at the balcony, where Willow was still beckoning.

Lord St. Ledger's box was a wooden structure with windows along one side through which the race course could be observed; a door led through the windowed wall to a balcony that ran the length of the stands and served all the private boxes, of which there were twenty. The box itself had all the charm of a cricket pavilion in winter, save for the imported items of comfort brought in by the St. Ledger servants. This consisted mainly of two dozen plain but comfortable chairs, their velveteen seats stuffed with horsehair, the dining table and its damask linen, and the crested china and silver. Tomorrow the boards would be bare, save for the spiders that would spin their webs happily until the next race meeting.

Bartlett led the way up the narrow wooden stairs, ignoring the two policemen who guarded the last landing from trespassers. Emilio followed, taking the steps two by two; Bellucci puffed along behind him. On entering the box, Emilio was confronted by a large man in a silk top hat, a dark grey tailcoat with grey silk lapels, striped trousers, and grey spats, beneath which black toe caps shone like polished jet.

Bartlett paused briefly to regain his breath. "Signor Scala and Signor Bellucci, my Lord."

St. Ledger held out an enthusiastic hand. "Now, tell me which one of you gentlemen is the luckiest man in the world."

Emilio took the big man's hand. "Me, sir. I win the Sweepstake. This is Bellucci, my friend."

Willow let them get on with the introductions before moving in. A steward brought a tray of freshly poured champagne. St. Ledger looked around the box to make sure that all of his guests were paying attention; being a noted sportsman and gambler, for some reason, he treasured this moment all most as much as meeting the boxer Big Jack O'Dea after his win on Epsom Downs.

"A toast, everyone, to the luckiest man in the world: Signor Emilio Scala."

The company, each in their own way, studied the Italian as they raised their glasses in answer to their host's instructions. Willow tipped hers directly at Emilio and approached him. St. Ledger saw her coming. "Ah. Willow, I believe you know each other."

"We've met. Congratulations. What you did took a lot of nerve.

You're more than just a lucky man."

Intrigued, St. Ledger asked, "May I ask what Signor Scala did that separates him from the rest of us mortals?"

Willow smiled seductively directly at Emilio. "He bravely turned down twenty-five thousand pounds for half of his ticket seconds before the race."

St. Ledger gave Emilio a genuine look of admiration. "You sound like a man who plays poker."

Bellucci took a drink from his bubbling glass, and butted in, "Si. He is a champion poker player. He won the Sweep ticket with a pair of twos. I saw him do it." Bellucci stopped talking and smiled proudly.

"Ah. A bluffer. We have a lot in common, Emilio; come, let me introduce you to my friends." St. Ledger guided Emilio across the box, where they took up conversation with Minnie Barton and Greville Hanson, leaving Willow with Bellucci, who was frantically going through his pockets.

"Have you lost something?" Willow inquired.

"Yes, I forgot in the excitement that I back Fantasy. I had a pound each way at two hundred to one. I win fifty pounds; now I can't find my ticket."

"You're a lucky pair, is that it?" Willow pointed to a corner of card that poked from Bellucci's waistcoat pocket.

Bellucci retrieved the card with a broad fat smile. "Si, si this is it." He waved the ticket in the air and shouted across the box. "Emilio, Emilio! I won fifty quid." He shook the ticket. "I back Fantasy just in case."

St. Ledger's guests watched the fat man in amazement as he jigged a little dance.

"I go now and get my money." He looked at Willow. "Can I come back in?"

Willow unpinned her badge and gave it to Bellucci. "Of course you can, just show this to the policemen."

Bellucci waddled out of the box. Willow joined Emilio and the group who pressed him for the winner of the next race, hoping that there was more luck left in the Italian's arsenal. Emilio, enjoying the attention, readily took on the role of an expert. He had put the overwhelmingly wonderful consequences of his win into a separate compartment of his consciousness, allowing himself to drift to the door of it occasionally, in the way one fondles a wrapped Christmas present and refrains from opening it until the appropriate time. For now, he was happy to indulge in this unique aspect of a day at the races.

Willow watched the handsome Italian. There was a new confidence about him, which was not entirely surprising as he was about to pocket a third of a million pounds. She had thought him attractive on their first meeting, but to take that thought any further had been out of the question. Now, of course, things were very different.

She saw an opportunity to catch St. Ledger as he looked at his race card and sidled up to him. "Bunkie, do invite Emilio to travel back with us on the train. It would be terrific fun to have him sit in at the poker game."

St.Ledger took an immediate liking to this idea. "Absolutely, it would be fun. I'll ask him."

St. Ledger strolled over to Emilio, His Lordship beamed with pleasure at having snaffled such a sporting celebrity into his party. "Emilio, we have a bit of a ritual on Grand National day; perhaps you would care to share it with us?"

Emilio looked a little bewildered.

"I have a private Pullman on the London train, and it would be my pleasure if you would consent to travel back with us. We play poker all the way back to Paddington, and then we shall dine at the Twenty-One Club. I would be honoured to host a celebration of your great good fortune."

Private Pullman, Twenty-One Club, poker, celebration; Emilio got the gist of His Lordship's invitation.

"Do come, Emilio, we'll have such a wonderful time," Willow insisted in her most seductive manner. There was something very exciting about this lucky man. He exuded an animal magnetism, a magnetism that Willow had decided to fully explore.

Emilio's first reaction was to make sure the invitation included his friend. "Bellucci as well?"

"Of course; that's settled then." St. Ledger gave Emilio a pat on the back and left him to Willow while he went in search of Bartlett. He found him hovering at the door of the box. "Bartlett, look, I want you to get to a telephone. Call that chap Moss who dresses everybody for balls and things when they're caught short in the wardrobe department. But first, I want you to ascertain, without causing any embarrassment, the measurements of Mr. Scala and his friend. They'll be dining with me at the Twenty One. Have Moss deliver suitable clothes for them to the Pullman when we reach Paddington."

Bartlett concealed his amazement and nodded. "I'll see to it right away, Milord."

"Oh, and Bartlett, send in the bookmaker. I think we're all ready for the next race."

Grant had left his boys to get on with the job of bookmaking. There was still a lot of money to be taken from this huge crowd on the next three races. In the bar at the top of the stands, surrounded by the cream of racing society, he did his arithmetic. He had managed to back Grakle to win one hundred and fifty grand. He had lost money on Gregalach, and as a result had no share in the Sweepstake's second prize. He did, however, have two thirds of the third prize, since Willow had bought a share in Fantasy. This would draw sixty six grand. He knocked back a scotch and continued scribbling with a pencil on his race card. Whichever way he worked the figures, Willow's scheme had cost him thirty-odd grand, plus the time and aggravation. He added the four grand that Willow had owed him in the first place, cursing at the thought of having forgotten that.

'Thirty-four grand in the hole, just 'cause I listened to some posh debutante's crazy scheme. It would have been bad enough, even if I had screwed her. She would have had to be very good to justify a thirty-four grand screw."

Without even this small conciliation, Grant felt gutted. It was with malice in his heart that he entered Lord St. Ledger's box to take the bets for the next race.

Grant ignored the tray of drinks offered by a steward; the day was not yet over. If he was to climb out of this mess, he would need to keep his wits about him. He went diligently to work with his little red book, taking bets from the St. Ledger guests.

Willow saw him and excused herself from the conversation she was having with Emilio and Greville. Moving across the room, she intercepted Grant between punters, just out of earshot of the rest of the company. "Well, Toby, how did we do?"

Toby Grant gave Willow a contemptuous look. Leaning forward he whispered. "You did very well, young lady. I did thirty-odd grand."

Willow inspected Toby's face for a sign that would suggest that he might be lying to her. She had only his word that he hadn't got the bets on. "I'm very disappointed in you, Toby. You told me that you could make a big bet, but you couldn't. The failure is yours. You've wasted a golden opportunity, and cost us both a lot of money."

She smiled at him for the sake of the approaching St. Ledger. Toby Grant managed to conceal his anger by writing something in his book.

"What have you backed? Lucky Emilio has tipped Thunder Dragon."

"He might have used up his good luck; I've had a small bet on Lodge Farm."

St. Ledger looked at his race card. "Lodge Farm, eh? Toby, what price for Thunder Dragon?"

Toby Grant lifted his binoculars to study the boards of the bookmakers down in the ring. His tic-tac man was signalling various changes in the betting. Toby watched him for a few moments until he was satisfied that he had the current betting picture. "It seems to have come in from tens to eight to one."

"I'll take that if it's moving. One thousand at eight to one. By the way, Toby, are you to grace us with your company on the train? I do believe there will be a respectable poker game to amuse us during the journey. That fellow over there has won the Sweepstake; I hope he will agree to play on my behalf. With, of course, an open purse. He might just be the luckiest man in the world, you know."

Toby Grant looked over to Emilio. "I would be delighted. But I have a friend with me; is there room for two of us?"

St. Ledger smiled broadly, his moustache lifting up into his cheeks. "If he has a bag full of money and is a friend of yours, he will be more than welcome; your friend will make the table up to six. Now, if you will excuse me."

St. Ledger took Willow's arm. "Come, my dear, shall we watch Thunder Dragon try to win this race?"

Toby Grant took his red book to the remaining guests. He congratulated Emilio in passing, with a manufactured smile. "Congratulations, Mr. Scala, you did very well. Will you be wanting to place a bet on this race?

Emilio looked at the bookmaker, guessing how he really felt. "No thank you. I think I have backed enough horses for one day. I shall watch this race."

Toby Grant continued on his journey around the box. As the white flag came down to start the fourth race of the day, he pushed his way through the crowd in the top terrace of the Aintree Grand Stand; turning left, he climbed six wooden steps, then turned right and walked through a swing door that had a sign above it which read, 'The Select Bar.' This bar was busy, but not as crushed as the rest of the racecourse.

Toby Grant made his way along the line of drinkers. He stopped behind a tall, immaculately dressed man. He'd found who he was searching for: his old friend Harry P. Valentine, poker player and master card sharp.

Lord St. Ledger's party left the box before the last race and made their way through the carnival crowd along the south side of the course to the waiting Pullman in Fazakerley station. Most of the occupants of the other private boxes would be making their way back to Liverpool's Grand Hotel for the annual Grand National Dinner, but Lord St. Ledger's guests would do no such thing.

Once in the Pullman, they settled down in the warmth and comfort of the most luxurious train carriage that money could buy. Silk curtains protected the occupants from the inquisitive eyes of any members of the public who tried to gaze through the bevelled glass windows. Twenty coats of lapis blue paint had gone in to the lustre of the exterior. It was a long Pullman with two bathrooms, both of which produced hot water. There was a fully equipped galley, from which guests would receive a regular supply of gourmet snacks. The main salon was decorated in French colonial style; dark red and lapis drapes hung from gilded fittings; numerous comfortable arm chairs and chaise longues occupied an area close to an ornate stove which heated bathwater and radiators, as well as throwing a comfortable glow into the salon itself. Further down the salon, separated slightly from the seating area by luscious drapes, was the octagonal card table, illuminated by a gas-lit chandelier.

Emilio had never seen anything like it. A high tea had been served almost immediately the moment the door of the carriage was closed, and Bellucci looked like the happiest man in the world; ten crisp fivers in his pocket and a side table groaning with delicious cakes within arm's reach—he was in heaven.

"You were right, Emilio. We won't forget this day."

He watched St. Ledger forking cake into his moustache-framed mouth, and made an attempt to copy his manners with a fork full of chocolate gateaux. Willow poured tea at this table, while Minnie Barton played hostess at a similar one across the carriage.

"You might as well make yourselves comfortable; the train won't leave for an hour or so. We will start the cards directly after tea," announced St. Ledger.

Sir John Bingham had had a bad day at the races, losing consistently. He rubbed his hands together impatiently, as if he was trying to get a flame from an aboriginal fire stick. "Gobble up, everybody, I'd like to recover some funds."

Miles Grenfell had avoided tea and cake in favour of a large brandy. He perked up at the prospect of some real action, bored with making small talk to His Lordship's floozies. "Hear! hear! Let's have some cards." He swigged his brandy, pacing about the salon restlessly. "Signor Scala, do you suppose that Italian poker rules are the same as ours—I mean, what beats what and all that?"

St. Ledger thought that this was a good point. "Quite right, Miles; we don't want any argy-bargy after you've lost a hand or so to our guest, do we? We would be wise to write down what beats what, then there will be no arguments. Bartlett, pen and paper."

Emilio and Bellucci had no need for a list of winning hands; Emilio recited his understanding of the rules as a bright schoolboy would his seven times table.

Satisfied that all was in order, St. Ledger turned to Emilio. "Emilio, I would be honoured if a man of your luck would take my cards for me. Unless, of course, you wish to play with your own money; I must warn you that these fellows insist on playing for fairly savage stakes. As you have so recently made a fortune, I presume you are not yearning to lose it?"

Emilio thought it strange that these people didn't like to ask a direct question. "Are you saying that you want me to play with your money?"

"Exactly. You play for me, and there will be no limit. If you lose, I pay; if you win, you will be rewarded by your very grateful host—what do you say?"

Bellucci liked this idea a lot, and said so before Emilio could answer. "You're a clever man; he's a great poker player, you see."

Emilio smiled with embarrassment. "Si, why not? I will enjoy to play for you, I hope I win."

"Good that's settled. Shall we adjourn, gentlemen?" St. Ledger addressed the girls. "Ladies, will you excuse us? The green baize beckons. Feel free to watch the game, as and when you please. Gentleman?"

Leaving the women to chat and discuss their day, St. Ledger ushered his guests through to the gaming compartment of the carriage. The octagonal green baize of the table glowed like a fine-cut emerald, framed by a broad band of highly polished marquetry. Each place had an inset channel of Moroccan leather to hold gaming chips.

Emilio took his seat, becoming aware of the voices of the Aintree crowd; the voices grew louder, rising to a crescendo as the winner of the last race of the day passed the winning post, only to diminish again to a faint murmur. Only the occasional shout penetrated the draped gas-lit seclusion of St. Ledger's carriage. Here Emilio Scala was sitting in the comfort of a king, while outside, racehorse owners, trainers, bookmakers and thousands of punters went about the business of trying to win. That's what they were all here for. They were all trying to win. Today Emilio Scala had done just that. Today he had become a master winner. He chuckled to himself. If DeMarco and the boys could see him now.

Emilio looked around, noticing the small things. Everything in here was perfect; the oil paintings on the wall, the braid and sashes on the drapes, the reflection of the gas light on the polished wooden surfaces. He put his hands palm-down on the cool smooth wood of the card table; the inlay was made so perfectly, like a priceless mandolin. This was what you did with money; this was where you put your wife—not in a yard with train smoke and a broom and dust, and red, chapped hands on a winter's morning.

'God willing, I will do this for my family; I will put them in a perfect place like this.'

Emilio was interrupted from his thoughts by Bartlett, who excused himself as he placed a quantity of beautiful chips into the inset leather box in front of him.

St. Ledger took a seat—not one of the table seats; they were reserved for players only—but a chair that Bartlett had produced behind Emilio and to his left. Bellucci was given a similar chair to Emilio's right. Miles Grenfell sat directly opposite Emilio. Sir John Bingham took a seat to Emilio's right that faced Greville Hanson. An empty chair separated each of the four players. Several decks of unopened linen cards lay neatly on the green baize. Greville took one and ran his thumb nail along the sixpenny stamp that sealed its box. With a practised shake, the waxy cards slipped into the palm of his left hand. Bartlett removed the empty box and the spare decks, as Greville shuffled.

"Gentlemen, may I suggest the stakes? Red chips, one hundred; blue, two hundred; red octagonals, five hundred; blue octagonals, one thousand; red plaques, five thousand; blue plaques, ten thousand. One hundred pounds to open, and no raise to be larger than the pot."

Greville continued to shuffle the cards while he spoke. He put the cards down for Emilio to cut. The cards felt cool to Emilio's touch.

Greville picked them up and announced, "Seven-card stud poker, gentlemen." He proceeded to deal.

Toby Grant had done well on the last three races; he had offered generous odds on the favourites, and they had all been beaten. While his boys paid out the stragglers, he using the depths of the big leather bookie's bag as cover as he counted the day's take. He bundled the notes together and flicked through them with a practised skill. His friend Harry P. Valentine smirked as he watched the bookmaker counting.

"That's good, lads, you did well; there's over seven grand in the bag—look after it well. We'll do the tally in the office in the morning. I'll be travelling back in the luxury of his Lordship's Pullman; now, don't get jealous, will you?" Toby's boys laughed at their boss's joke. "Now, pay off the tic-tac man and be on your way, and don't take your eyes off that bag."

Toby and Harry P. Valentine made their way along the course to Fazakerley Station. The lapis-blue carriage glowed like a sapphire in the evening winter sun. They watched the hordes squeezing into the ordinary carriages as they walked across the track to the spur on which the Pullman was waiting.

Harry P. Valentine stopped to put a cigarette into an amber holder with a thin gold band around the rim. Toby lit it for him.

"I'll probably be able to give you one good shot; it'll come from my deal. Take the first available seat to the Italian's right. I'll find my own seat," said the card sharp with confidence.

Toby put his lighter away. "How will I know when you've fixed the hand?"

"Watch me deal; if the forefinger of my left hand protrudes from behind the deck as I deal, start betting." To make sure that Toby understood, Harry P. Valentine showed him with an imaginary deal. "Got it?"

"Got it."

"Good. There will only be one chance, and you'll have to take it."

"Fair enough, Harry. This wop has cost me a lot of money."

Harry P. Valentine gave Toby a quizzical look. "One more thing, Toby: three grand or twenty-five percent of the pot. Whichever is greater, that's my cut, okay?"

"Okay, but remember you're not there to play for yourself; his Lordship is a very valued client. I'll be guaranteeing you, so I don't want you to win and I don't want you to lose; just do the job, and the three grand—possibly more—is yours."

A young steward, on seeing the two men approach, opened the carriage door and lowered the folding steps. "Good evening, Mr. Grant. His Lordship is expecting you." The steward held the door open for the guests.

"Who's winning?"

"I believe Mr. Scala is, sir; he's having a very lucky day."

"We'll see about that," said Toby, handing the steward his coat.

Harry P. Valentine did the same, revealing an immaculately cut suit of dark blue worsted with the thinnest of red stripes running through it. Harry eyed the ladies as he entered the salon. "Very nice," he said to himself as he caught site of Minnie Barton's crossed ankles.

Willow almost dropped her cup at the sight of Toby crossing the thick carpet in her direction with his hand held out. "Good evening, Willow, have you had a good day?" he said facetiously.

"Oh, very good, thank you, Toby."

"So have I, so have I. May I introduce you to Mr. Harry P. Valentine. Willow Rutherford. I'm afraid I haven't had the pleasure of being formally introduced to the other ladies."

Willow introduced the girls.

"What does the P. stand for, Mr. Valentine?" asked the slightly tipsy Minnie.

"Peregrine, Miss Barton."

The girls giggled. Harry didn't like their irreverence. "Well! Shall we play cards, Toby? It's been a pleasure to meet you." He bowed slightly and followed Toby towards the sound of clinking poker chips and the smell of cigar smoke.

Bartlett bent low to whisper in His Lordship's ear, "Mr. Grant and his friend have arrived, Milord; shall I show them in?"

St. Ledger momentarily tore his eyes away from the table; Emilio had just seen Sir John's hand for three thousand pounds. Sir John turned over his cards: a pair of kings and little else. Emilio showed his two pairs and took the pot.

St. Ledger smiled broadly, making his moustache jump up into his cheeks. "Show them in. We have fresh blood, gentlemen."

The players looked up at the new arrivals as Toby introduced his friend to St. Ledger, who in turn introduced the newcomers to the table. "You've arrived just in time. Signor Scala's luck seems to be holding out; he's playing for me, in case you wondered why I'm not sitting in. Take your seats, gentlemen."

Toby took the vacant seat between Emilio and Sir John. Harry P. Valentine took the seat to Emilio's left, and immediately scrutinised his fellow players, looking for the signs of a wise man among them. His immediate reading was favourable; he could tell a lot from the way players greeted newcomers into the game. He was pleased to note that all the players had the mark of compulsive gamblers as opposed to hard-core profit takers; he also knew that it was far too early to make any hard judgements. He sniffed the wonderful smell of Moroccan leather and polished wood that lay sweetly under the cigar smoke. "Chips, please." Hhe raised a finger.

Miles Grenfell sipped his brandy and took it upon himself to explain the values of the chips and plaques, laying them neatly on the green baize in front of him.

"I'll start with five thousand in that case. Toby?

Toby Grant agreed. "Yes, five thousand, that should get us started."

Bartlett laid five thousand pounds' worth of the coloured lozenges in front of each of the newcomers. Harry P. Valentine made stacks of his rather than laying them in the purpose-built tray; just as he had arranged them neatly, the carriage lurched forward with a bump, spilling them symmetrically onto the green baize. The brandy in all the glasses rocked in little waves.

"Don't panic; we've just been connected up to the London train and will be on the move very soon."

Harry restacked his chips as he watched Emilio shuffle and deal the next hand.

The train eventually pulled out of Fazakerley Station, and the game settled down to the accompaniment of the rhythmic sound of steel wheels speeding over steel rails. Periodically the girls drifted in to watch the game, which progressed with varying degrees of excitement. Bellucci spent his time keeping a mental note of Emilio's winnings, which now stood at approximately fifteen thousand pounds, mostly taken from Sir John, who had twice called for more chips. Miles Grenfell was a little ahead, Greville Hanson was losing, and Toby and Harry P. Valentine seemed to be holding their own.

The game had been in progress for an hour or so when Toby suggested that his Lordship might prefer to play rather than watch. This thought had crossed St. Ledger's mind, even though Emilio was making him a nice profit.

In between deals and while Greville Hanson was shuffling the cards, Toby sipped his brandy and looked directly at Emilio. "It's a pity we aren't going to get a crack at that new-found fortune of yours. I suppose these stakes are a bit rich for you."

Emilio gave Toby a look that confirmed his dislike for the bookmaker. Miles Grenfell, who liked a bit of friction, agreed. "It does make for a more interesting game when one's risking one's own money."

St. Ledger came to Emilio's defence. "Emilio doesn't have any money. It will be weeks before he receives his prize."

St. Ledger had given Toby the opening he had been looking for. "His credit is good enough for me; if he should lose, I'd be pleased to except his I.O.U."

Emilio kept calm; there was nothing he would like more than to take the bookmaker the way he had taken DeMarco in the game that had started all this. But he had committed himself to play for his Lordship.

St. Ledger sensed Emilio's predicament and gave him an opportunity to get off the hook. "Emilio, if you would prefer to play for yourself, it's perfectly all right with me. I'm sure your credit is good with all these gentlemen."

Bellucci was not happy with this development. He knew what a stubborn bastard his friend was. He also knew that behind the calm-looking exterior, Emilio was dying to get into the game for himself, Bellucci prayed that he wouldn't. Emilio counted up the chips in front of him, making stacks of one thousand pounds—twenty-one of them in all.

That made a profit of sixteen thousand for his Lordship. Emilio slid the stacks across the table to St. Ledger. "If it's okay with you, I'd love to play for myself."

St. Ledger moved around the table and took the empty seat between Greville Hanson and Miles Grenfell. He pulled most of the stacks of chips towards himself, leaving five stacks behind; these he pushed back to Emilio. "Spoils for the warrior, Emilio. Now you have a stake."

Bellucci looked pleased. Willow occupied the seat that St. Ledger had vacated at Emilio's left elbow. "I won't make you nervous if I sit here, will I?"

Emilio looked at the beautiful Willow, so close to him. "Not at all. You will steel my nerve and bring me luck."

Sir John picked up the spent cards and, with the grumpy tone of a loser, demanded a fresh deck. Bartlett brought one and took the old cards away.

The carriage had been stationary for some time now. The solitary Pullman parked in its siding at Paddington station looked dark and empty, save for wisps of smoke that drifted from its chimneystack, and the odd chink of light that shone through little gaps in the curtains. Inside, the poker game was still very much in progress.

Headlights lit up the siding, and a car crunched along the shingle by the side of the tracks, stopping at the Pullman. The driver got out, carrying two large boxes. He knocked on the door, which was immediately opened by a steward.

The car driver lifted the boxes. "Is this St. Ledger's Pullman?"

"That's right."

"I've got a delivery here from Moss Brothers, the tailors."

"That's right; we've been expecting you." The steward gave the driver a shilling and took the boxes inside. Bartlett came through to examine the contents.

At the table, Harry P. Valentine had won the last game; he picked up the spent cards with skilful, practised fingers and shuffled them a few times while they lay flat on the table, then boxed them up, cut them, and shuffled them again, leaving the two halves on the table and letting the cards run together by running his thumbs up their edges. He did this twice, pushed the cards together, and picked up the deck. He then made two quick shuffles by letting the cards fall from one hand to the other and gave the deck to Emilio to cut, he then proceeded to deal. He dealt around the table anti clockwise, giving each player a single card with its face to the green baize before finally dealing one to himself. He repeated the process, paused briefly and did the same again; this time he dealt the card face up on the table.

Sir John opened for a thousand pounds, and the six other players came in. Emilio had felt a tingle of pleasure travel down his spine as he looked at his dark cards: two red sixes in the hole, and the six of spades laying face-up on the table. Three of a kind. He had been content to match Sir John's opening bet and resisted the urge to raise him; he would wait to see what other surprises this hand had in store.

Harry P. Valentine's nimble fingers dealt the fourth card. He dealt a red eight to Emilio, and Toby Grant improved his hand. He now showed a pair of jacks next to his two dark cards. Toby opened for two thousand pounds. Sir John showed an ace and a seven, and came in. Miles Grenfell folded. St. Ledger, who had a nine in the hole and a nine on the table, came in for two thousand. Hanson was ace high; he decided to stay in for one more card.

Harry P. Valentine slid his two thousand into the pot and dealt the fifth card. He gave Emilio the six of clubs, Toby the two of diamonds, and Sir John drew another seven. Grenfell, St. Ledger, and Harry P. Valentine did not improve. Toby's two jacks still looked good. He opened for three thousand pounds, sliding the chips into the pot. Sir John took the bet, hoping to improve on his pair of sevens. St. Ledger bet, hoping to better his pair of nines with the next two cards. Hanson and Harry P. Valentine folded.

Emilio, confident that his showing pair of sixes looked inadequate in this game, resisted the temptation to raise the bet; he pushed in the required amount from his remaining chips into the table. This left him with exactly three hundred pounds—hardly enough to remain in the game without taking up the offer of credit. At this point, the remaining players had contributed seven thousand pounds each into the pot. Harry P. Valentine dealt the sixth card of the hand, and the last open one to the remaining players.

He gave the eight of hearts to Emilio; this gave him two pairs showing. This delighted Emilio, although he showed no sign. He could now raise any bet made on the strength of two pairs without signalling the excellence of his four sixes.

Toby received the two of clubs; he now also had two pairs showing with jacks high. Sir John and St. Ledger did not improve but waited to see what Toby Grant would bet.

Toby looked at his diminished pile of chips; like Emilio he had seven thousand in the pot and a few hundred in his tray. He raised a finger to attract Bartlett. The butler needed no attracting; he was well aware of the state of play. Bartlett bent to receive Toby's whispered command. He took a number of plaques from the chip box, together with a note pad and pen, and gave them to Toby, who took them and signed the paper.

"I'll open for five thousand pounds."

Toby slid a five thousand red plaque into the pot. Sir John threw his cards onto the table in disgust. "Pass," he said dejectedly.

St. Ledger fiddled with his cards for a moment; then, flicking them into the table, he moaned, "Pass," angry at having been pushed out of such a good pot.

Emilio studied Toby Grant's cards, then his face. There was danger on the table. Emilio struggled hard to know if it was he who was in danger or the bookmaker. He motioned to Bartlett in the same manner that he had seen the other do when requiring more ammunition. Bartlett was there in a flash with chips and the note pad.

"I raise you five thousand." Emilio pushed ten thousand pounds into the pot.

Bellucci almost gasped. A sort of fire of excitement flashed in Willow's eyes. The other players seemed to squirm with anticipation as Toby Grant considered his bet.

Toby Grant separated his cards with a forefinger. Mentally, he estimated the amount in the pot: nearly sixty grand, and one more card to play; if he played this right and didn't scare the Italian off, he could crunch him with the next bet. Modestly, he slid chips to the value of five thousand pounds into the pot.

Harry P. Valentine had skilfully done his job. All that remained for him was to watch the outcome; so far he felt that Toby had played it just right. He dealt the final and dark card. Grant was clever; he picked up his card with just the right amount of anxiety. Emilio saw what he was meant to see and felt confident. He looked at his last dark card, hoping to give the impression that it was important to him. Then Toby made his bet. "Ten thousand pounds."

Toby sat back in his chair; this was his only mistake. Emilio didn't like the way he did it, and a sort of paranoia crept over him. He hadn't liked Harry P. Valentine since he first sat down. There had been something about the way he played that disturbed Emilio; he didn't feel that he had been playing to win. Quite suddenly, alarm bells began to ring in his head. Harry P. Valentine had dealt this hand. Emilio had in full confidence been about to raise the bet from ten thousand to the pot limit: a bet approaching eighty thousand pounds. He, after all, faced two pairs with a disguised four sixes. He had often dreamed of such a hand. Was his paranoia justified? It would cost him ten grand to see Toby Grant's hand.

There was complete silence at the table as Emilio wrestled with his dilemma. He desperately wanted to raise the bookmaker's bet.

Grant sat, watching and waiting, praying that the Italian would raise him. Keeping a poker face, he sat it out.

"See you." Emilio said it quite matter-of-factly as he pushed ten thousand pounds worth of chips into the pot.

Toby Grant cursed under his breath. He showed his hand to the table by turning over his dark cards. A barely audible sound came from the other players and the spectators as the four Jacks were revealed. Emilio didn't show his hand; he simply turned his cards face down on the green baize and slid them into the discards. The room burst into chatter.

Willow leaned over to Emilio. "What did you have?"

He looked at her as if to say, 'You shouldn't ask a man a question like that,' and said. "A losing hand, Bella, a losing hand.

Grant raked in his winnings as Emilio watched, confident that the cheating had not been detected or at least could not be proven. Harry P. Valentine knew Emilio had twigged that something was wrong; any normal gambler would have raised into two pairs when holding a concealed four of a kind. He wondered where he had gone wrong, but quickly dismissed this thought—he knew he was too good—and mentally laid the blame of the failure on Toby Grant.

Lord St. Ledger stood up. "I think we will call it a day, gentlemen; if you'll excuse me, I shall dress for dinner." St. Ledger left the table to go to his bath-come-dressing room.

Bartlett took charge of the tally, giving each of the players any notes that they had signed during the course of the game. Emilio signed an I.O.U. to Toby Grant for fifteen thousand pounds.

"It could have been much worse," said Emilio knowingly.

Grant ignored what he knew was a "You cheated me, you bastard" look. He thanked Emilio and pocketed the I.O.U. "I'll see you on payday, Signor Scala. Have a good night out with his Lordship."

Toby Grant and Harry P. Valentine stepped down from the carriage onto the shingle of the siding; they would walk through the station to the taxi rank.

Emilio hadn't hit a man with his full strength for nearly twenty years, but if the bookmaker had stayed another minute, he would have changed all that.

Instead he turned away to see Bartlett approaching, carrying two cardboard boxes. "Mr. Scala, if you would follow me, I have a change of clothes for you and Mr. Bellucci, as you will be required to dress for dinner. If you will put your own clothes in the boxes, I will see that the driver takes them in the car with you."

Bellucci looked puzzled as he followed Emilio to the dressing room. Once inside, Emilio was conspicuously silent. Bellucci was dying to speak but waited until Bartlett had laid out the clothes and left the room; as soon as the door was closed Bellucci let fly with a stream of curses, then got more specific. "Emilio Scala, you are a fucking idiot. Those guys cheat you and you don't see it; what's a matter with you?"

Emilio had taken of his jacket and shirt and was washing his face. "Listen, I was lucky I didn't lose a fortune. I was ready to raise the bastard the pot. I was sitting on four sixes, and I could see nothing to beat me in his hand. Even the way he bet, I wasn't sure. Clever bastards."

"What are you going to do about it?"

"What can I do about it? Nothing. I can't prove anything. You think this is the wild fucking west? I gotta go and shoot them?" Emilio dried his face.

"Are you going to tell his Lordship St. Ledger?"

"No I do nothing, that's it; it's my own fault. No more gambling. Nazarena is right, I'm fucking stupid. Okay? I don't want to hear any more. Okay?"

Bellucci agreed. "Okay."

He took off his jacket and shirt and began to wash himself, while Emilio examined the hired clothes. Emilio held the evening suit up under his chin. "Hey, Bellucci, look at this."

Bellucci looked up with a soap-covered face to see Emilio doing a little dance while holding the suit against his chest. "Come on, shave that beard off and let's have some fun. We're rich! So I lose a bit. Anyway, Willow is waiting for me to dance with her."

Bellucci pinched his nose with thumb and forefinger, lifting it high and revealing a fat bobbing Adam's apple; waving the open razor, he pretended to cut his throat. Emilio continued to dance, holding the evening suit as if it were his partner.

# CHAPTER NINETEEN

Nazarena wasn't listening to the swirling sound of the piano accordion that filled the café. For the umpteenth time, she pulled aside the makeshift curtain that Scippio had rigged up to afford the occupants of the café some privacy from the prying eyes of the vast crowd of public and press that had now firmly camped on the pavement outside. The curly hands of the station clock now stood at ten past eight. A flashbulb burst like an exploding sun through the glass window, inches from her face; she dropped the curtain, frightened and temporarily blinded, and started to cry.

Selma came to her rescue, putting an arm around her and holding her close to her ample young bosom. "Nazarena, don't worry. It's a long way, Liverpool. He will be home soon."

Nazarena made more of her sobbing as her friend held her. "It's that fancy woman with silk stockings; he's with her. I saw his face, and that Bellucci—they get drunk and miss the train."

Bellucci's mother, in her black shawl, sat crocheting a small circle of lace; she hardly looked up, understanding the situation completely. "Don't be stupid; so what? Enjoy yourself. You win a fortune, non essere pieno di miseria. Enjoy yourself." The old woman shouted across the room. "Umberto, vieni! Sing her a song."

Umberto, rosy with vino, plucked away deliriously on his mandolin and had to be nudged out of his trance by other partygoers. He made his way across the room to comply with the old woman's request. He chose a little song about a cockerel who lost his way to the hen house, singing the first line a capella; then he came in with the mandolin. Everybody in the room sang the well-known chorus. Umberto was a good minstrel, and by the second chorus, Nazarena—half-crying and half-laughing—joined in.

# CHAPTER TWENTY

The Twenty-One Club was one of those establishments that exist in any metropolis at any time, catering to the rich, the successful, and the decadent of a city's population. Entry was strictly at the discretion of the Russian owner, Prince Oscar Obolenski, who commanded that wonderful skill of mixing riffraff with the social establishment. The place, housed in a Piccadilly basement, literally glittered from the refracted crystal light of its many chandeliers, shaded here and there by potted palms and discreet screens. The orchestra, in white suits with satin lapels, pumped out a continuous stream of well-played dance music, with occasional songs from the handsome black brilliantined conductor. The small but adequate dance floor filled and emptied at the beginning and end of each song, confirming to Oscar Obolenski that he was not overpaying the bandleader.

With much fawning and flattery, the St. Ledger party were guided to the Twenty-One's best table. Bellucci caught sight of Emilio's reflection in one of the many mirrors and nudged him. "Paesane, you look like a film star. Me, how I look?"

Emilio appraised his fat friend for a moment. "You look like Don Bellucci, capo dei capi of Battersea."

St. Ledger stopped the flower girl as she wiggled by with a tray full of carnations, roses, and orchids; selecting an orchid, he had the girl pin it to Willow's dress.

Emilio and Bellucci surveyed the scene. The opulence and rowdy behaviour of the clientele stunned them into silence. They watched a magnum of champagne emptied into tall glasses that littered the linen-covered table, at the head of which Lord St. Ledger reigned supreme. Emilio peered across a giant flower arrangement at Willow; how could he talk to her across this table?

Bellucci, head swivelling in his starched white collar, scanned the sights in the room. On a balcony above the dance floor, a young drunk amused his friends by conducting the orchestra. Miles Grenfell leaned back in his chair, talking to the people at the next table, who in turn seemed to be inspecting Emilio. Sir John had apparently decided that Minnie Barton was his best bet for the evening and was busy charming her.

St. Ledger took a long drink of champagne, and looked in Emilio's direction. "Emilio, that was an unfortunate last hand. They do say that we punters can't beat the bookmakers. What's the next thing you will do with your money?"

Emilio sipped his drink. "I will send a telegram to Mussolini to tell him that there is another Italian who is doing well."

Those at the table who were listening laughed at the remark, particularly St. Ledger, who thought this very amusing. "What a good idea; let's send it now." St. Ledger snapped his fingers for a waiter, who was almost instantly at his side. "We wish to send a telegram; would you bring a form and a pen?"

The waiter vanished as quickly as he had appeared. "Now then, what are you going to say to him?"

Witty suggestions came from all parts of the table and from Grenfell's friends at the next. Emilio didn't understand most of the suggestions; then he realised that he was being ribbed. He stood up and raised his glass. "You think I make a big joke? Well, Mussolini, I bet he no make three hundred and fifty thousand pounds in one day. Chin Chin." Emilio drained his glass, to the amusement of the table.

The music stopped, and the coloured bandleader tapped his microphone with his baton. "My lords, ladies, gentlemen, and people of the night, I would like you to put your hands together for a newcomer to your illustrious ranks, the man who has today won the most amazing fortune—the first prize of the Irish Sweepstake, Signor Emilio Scala; give him a big hand."

The whole nightclub erupted into rapturous applause. A second magnum came to the table, as did a hoard of well-wishers. St. Ledger delighted in the proceedings. The orchestra struck up their own version of 'For He's a Jolly Good Fellow.'

As the entire nightclub sang the song, Prince Obolenski waddled his huge bulk through the crowd, followed by a waiter on whose tray, frozen into a block of ice, was a large bottle of pink vodka and an ample silver dish of beluga caviar, which he flamboyantly presented to a surprised Emilio. The orchestra slid smoothly into a tango, which allowed the party to really take off. Two stunning tipsy young flappers, undertaking a dare by their escorts at an adjacent table, pushed their squealing way to the table and attempted to seduce Emilio and Bellucci on to the dance floor.

Emilio knocked back the celebration vodka and stood up. Ignoring the advances of the flappers, he bowed to Willow. "May I have the honour of this dance?"

While Bellucci was being dragged to the dance floor, Emilio walked around the table, took Willow by the hand, and led her into a tango. To the surprise of the onlookers, Emilio cut a surprising step on the floor. In the circus, years ago, the daughters of Bandini had taught him well. He danced with great style and subtlety, his right hand lightly resting on Willow's lower spine, his left hand leading her into exciting swoops and turns.

Emilio felt the firmness of her body through the silk of her dress. The brush of her thigh against his had his blood pumping through his veins, and the sweet scent of her perfume went to his head. Lost in a dance of ecstasy, the floor was theirs.

The dance turned into an exhibition as the other dancers gradually cleared the floor to watch the luckiest man in the world at the height of his powers. As the tune ended, Emilio found himself with the beautiful Willow in his arms, surrounded by applauding people.

"Where did you learn to dance like that?" Willow asked breathlessly.

The orchestra went into a quickstep. Emilio squeezed Willow ever so slightly. "Now we do a quick step."

Other dancers moved back onto the floor; the ecstatic moment was over, leaving Emilio with a lingering feeling of masculine joy. He danced with Willow proudly until the quick step came to an end, then guided her back to the table to be greeted with compliments from the other guests.

St. Ledger was as busy as a schoolboy; he sat composing amusing messages to Benito Mussolini on blank telegram forms, reading the contents to his guests for approval. After several more shots of the frozen vodka, the table settled for a short, unfunny message, which Emilio approved, and a waiter took it away to have it sent to the Italian dictator.

St. Ledger, feeling a little bored at his lack of progress with Willow and now feeling the effect of Prince Obolenski's vodka, suggested a change of scene. The suggestion was whispered to the men, as the next venue was to be the exclusive brothel of the ex-music hall star, Betty Wilding.

Miles Grenfell and Greville Hanson decided to stay at the Twenty-One and joined the adjacent table; Mini Barton and the other girls stayed with them. St. Ledger, Sir John, Emilio, and Bellucci escorted Willow from the club, guided to the exit by the beaming prince.

"It is always a pleasure to see you Bunkie, enjoy what remains of the evening." The portly prince turned to Emilio, holding out his hairy tarantula of a hand. "Signor Scala, it has been a real pleasure to meet you; you are a lucky man. I hope you will visit us again."

Emilio shook the prince's hand as they crossed the red-carpeted lobby and through the heavy polished door.

The St. Ledger limousine waited at the curb of the Piccadilly pavement. It was one o'clock in the morning; the neon lights flashed on the buildings of the circus, and people congregated under the statue of Eros, who seemed to point his deadly little arrow directly at Emilio as he crossed the pavement and climbed into the Rolls-Royce. Willow squeezed in next to him. Bellucci took a front seat next to the chauffeur.

St. Ledger and Sir John lit cigars; the blue-scented smoke soon filled the car as it cruised down the Haymarket and turned on to St. James's Street, where it came to a halt at the black shining door of number eleven. St. Ledger was first out, followed by Sir John and Bellucci. Emilio waited for Willow to climb out.

"Good night, Emilio. I really enjoyed sharing your special day with you."

Emilio looked surprised. "Aren't you coming with us?"

Willow pulled her fur collar tightly to her throat. "No, no, this place is for boys only; it's well past my bed time."

A confused Emilio looked into her eyes. "Why you no stay with me? We have such a good time; don't go home." Emilio stood on the pavement, the chauffeur next to him holding the limousine door.

"Good night Emilio."

The chauffeur closed the door. Emilio stood looking through the window. Willow wound it down. "Come here."

Emilio moved forward, and Willow reached through the window. Taking him by the ear, she gently pulled his face close to hers and kissed him full on the lips. Emilio stood transfixed, savouring the taste of her delicious mouth, oblivious to the calls of Bellucci; he wanted more of her, to get closer to this smooth pale creature.

Willow took her face away from his quite abruptly, leaving Emilio in shock; she slipped a card into his hand. "If you like me, call me." She fell back in the leather comfort of the limousine. "Belgrave Square."

The Rolls-Royce silently pulled away, leaving a stunned Emilio standing on the pavement.

The black polished door with its large brass knocker was open as Emilio crossed the pavement to join his friends, who were already inside. A large turbaned black man took their coats. They were in a hall with a high ceiling, hung with brass lanterns set with coloured-glass windows through which gaslight filtered onto the walls and the Persian carpet on the stone floor. The black man padded away to a bead-curtained cloakroom, his curly-toed backless slippers flapping against the pink soles of his feet as he went.

St. Ledger led his friends through the hall into the main salon, reminiscent of a caliph's palace. The walls were draped in brocade; a fountain decorated with coloured tiles tinkled jets of water into a pool in which a few koi carp swam aimlessly about. Several well-dressed gentlemen reclined in comfortable ottoman chairs, drinks in hand, leisurely chatting to a dozen or so pretty girls. Beautiful carpets covered the tiled floor.

A handsome big-busted middle-aged woman wearing an embroidered caftan and exotic jewellery swooped on the newcomers. "Bunkie, where on earth have you been? I was beginning to think that you had taken your custom somewhere else."

St. Ledger took her offered hand and kissed it. "Where else could I go except to heaven, or possibly hell? Betty. I've brought a couple of friends along for a bit of entertainment." St. Ledger introduced the two bewildered Italians. Emilio, still reeling from Willow's farewell kiss, was trying hard to take this new environment in. "Betty! Signor Scala is celebrating. Today he won the Irish Sweepstake, and I am showing him the town."

"Congratulations!" the woman shrieked in a well-practiced theatrical manner, designed to encourage curiosity from her other guests. "Signor Scala, I heard about you on the radio. You have come to the perfect place." She turned to Sir John. "Sir John, how nice to see you. I've got someone special for you; she has just arrived from France. Come and meet the girls."

Betty led the foursome across the salon to a draped alcove, where deep-cushioned sofas surrounded an exquisite marquetry coffee table. "There, make yourselves comfortable while I organise the girls."

An Arab boy in slippers and baggy silk trousers silently laid out glasses. Bellucci and Emilio sank into one of the comfortable ottomans.

St. Ledger leaned across, puffing on his cigar, the smell of which mingled with the incense that floated in a thin blue plume from a brass container that hung above the fountain. "Emilio, have you ever been to a place like this?"

Emilio shook his head as he looked around at the various decorations. He watched a massive red and blue cockatoo eat grapes while hanging upside down from a hoop suspended from the ceiling. One of the girls fed him, to the amusement of her companion. "No. Never. What do we do?"

"Anything you like, my dear fellow. Anything you like," he laughed.

Betty returned with four fabulous-looking girls and the black boy, who brought a magnum of champagne to the table. He popped the cork and filled all the glasses. The girls sat down next to the men. Bellucci, now quite drunk, tried to sit up from the depths of the copious cushioned seat; the dark-haired girl next to him put her hand on his shoulder and pushed him gently back into his reclining position, then handed him a glass of champagne. In a thick foreign accent, she introduced herself. "My name is Esmeralda, and yours?"

Bellucci took the glass. "Bellucci. Alphonso Bellucci."

"Do you like me, Alphonso?" Esmeralda inquired.

Bellucci looked at Emilio for support. Emilio shrugged and smiled.

"Si. You are beautiful."

Esmeralda sat on the edge of his ottoman. "Good. Then we become very good friends."

An Amazonian redhead that Betty had chosen for St. Ledger introduced herself. St. Ledger put down his cigar and looked up at the giant creature. Obviously well pleased, he stood up. "No point in wasting time. I'll see you gentlemen later in the Turkish bath. Have a good time." He turned to the Amazon. "Boadicea, show me the way to your boudoir."

Sir John found himself sitting with a petite Indonesian girl from one of the French colonies. She took away his cigar and gave him his drink. She crossed her beautifully formed tiny legs, revealing her thigh to the hip through the slit in her silk oriental gown, and smiled at him in silence.

Emilio's girl looked like a Spanish gypsy; long black hair tumbled over her bare shoulders and down her back onto her scarlet dress. "If you don't like me, I will find you someone else."

Emilio looked at Bellucci, who was grinning from ear to ear. Getting no support from his blissed-out friend, he was forced to answer her, though his mind was still on the lingering kiss of Willow. "No, I like you very much, I just have never done, er... Been here before."

"My name is Consuela. When you know me, I am sure you will come back."

Sir John took his leave and disappeared with his oriental doll through the drapes of the salon, leaving Emilio and Bellucci to fend for themselves. Bellucci drained his glass and rocked his fat frame out of the comfortable ottoman. Esmeralda took his hand and helped him to his feet. As Esmeralda led him away, he turned his fat grinning face to Emilio. "Is this place really true?"

Emilio pulled a face and shrugged. "I think so." He watched his friend disappear through the drapes, then sat in silence, sipping his champagne—and trying hard not to look at Consuela.

"You don't want me, do you?"

Emilio felt embarrassed; he didn't want her, what he wanted was Willow. Then he thought of his innocent little wife waiting for her husband to come home from the races with hundreds of thousands of pounds. He suddenly felt really guilty. "You must understand I am a married man, I never do this before."

Consuela took his hand. "It's all right. We don't have to do anything. Your friend Lord St. Ledger will pay for my time anyway. Come, I will take you to the Turkish bath. I will make you relax while we wait for your friends."

Consuela pulled Emilio to his feet and led him through the drapes and down a stone staircase into a vaulted basement. Several rooms decorated with carved Moorish arches led into each other. Consuela led Emilio through a labyrinth of rooms. The place was enormous; it was hard to believe that all this was just a short way from Piccadilly. They went from room to room, passing several small pools, each occupied by two or three people. The further they went, the steamier and more scented the atmosphere grew, until Consuela opened a door to a dressing room. She slipped from her dress and hung it on a hook, then helped Emilio out of his clothes.

"Don't be shy, I am not going to eat you." She took off his jacket and his shirt. "Does my nakedness embarrass you?" She took a large towel and wrapped it around herself. "There, here is one for you."

She held out a towel, Emilio stepped out of his trousers and wrapped it around his now-naked body. She hung up his clothes, then took his hand led him through an arched door into a room full of steam.

At first, Emilio could see nothing, but as he acclimatised to the surroundings, he noticed a sort of stone table in the centre of the room. Consuela led him to it. The steam was hot; he felt it eat into his body as she took off his towel and made him lie down on the warm stone. "You lie there; I will be back shortly."

Emilio did as he was told. The vodka and the champagne had lifted his senses into a sort of dreamlike state. He wondered what he was doing in this strange place with this very nice young girl? Still guilt-ridden, he tried to relax, but Nazarena kept creeping in to his dream state. He knew that he should really be at home with his wife. The adventurous side of him, however, wanted to see this night through.

Consuela returned, carrying a bucket from which she took a thick raffia brush, like a huge shaving brush. She fanned it over Emilio's body, causing the heat of the steam to increase. Consuela was highly skilled; by fanning the brush, she focused heat on to specific parts of Emilio's body. He felt his body burn with pleasure as she fanned him; then quite suddenly, she plunged the giant brush on to his chest. It was full of a soapy substance that foamed as she applied it expertly to his entire body in long sweeping strokes, stopping occasionally to fan him again, increasing the heat to almost unbearable levels. Just as he thought he might scream with pain, she instinctively plunged the brush back onto the heated skin. This cooled him immediately, and the pleasure was almost intolerable.

She worked on him from head to toe until he lay relaxed and cleaner than he had ever been, breathing gently on the warm stone slab. Then with her hands, she began to massage him starting with his toes, then his feet. Occasionally he felt the tips of her firm breasts touch him as she reached across to take hold of another limb. Sometimes her sweet-smelling hair trickled across his face. She worked until he was consumed with a physical pleasure, and then she left him. He lay there, halfway between heaven and hell, almost sleeping but very much awake, until he realised that there were other people in the room. He opened his eyes and through the steam, he saw the familiar shape of his fat friend wrapped in a towel, standing over him. He sat up and swung his legs off the table.

"Consuela told me you were in here; how you feel?"

"Incredible, and you?"

Bellucci danced about in the steam. "Mamma mia, Esmeralda, que bella!"

Emilio slowly came to his senses and could now see quite clearly. He walked over to a stainless-steel shower and stood under the needles of ice-cold water. Bellucci joined him. "Where are St. Ledger and Sir John?"

"They are in the pool outside. I think these guys are crazy—they are going to have some more girls. For me, one Esmeralda is enough for a life time." Bellucci started dancing about again and singing his new love's name. "Esmeralda, Esmeralda."

"Come on, Bellucci, we gotta go home. She gonna murder me."

Bellucci stopped dancing. "You're right; she murder me, too. You watch, I get the blame. Anyway, you can do what you like now you're a rich man."

"That's what you think. Come on, let's go."

The two men left the steam room. They found St. Ledger and Sir John languishing in a hot pool. "Ah. Emilio, there you are. Did you enjoy yourself?"

"I did, Bunkie. That was very interesting. Now I have to leave you; my wife will be going mad with worry."

"The night is still young, Emilio. Stay for breakfast."

"No. No, we must go. Thank you very much for everything, I have had a fantastic day. Thank you."

St. Ledger lay up to his chin in the steaming pool. "If you're sure you won't stay, very well. It's been a pleasure meeting you. Don't forget now, if you need any advice investing your nice new money, you will get in touch with me, won't you?"

Emilio and Bellucci, wrapped in their towels, waved goodbye. Bellucci stopped Emilio and whispered. "Eh, where are our clothes? We can't go home in those monkey suits."

Emilio thought for a moment. "They are in the boot of the Rolls-Royce." He turned back to the pool, and looking a little embarrassed asked, "Excuse me, Bunkie, do you know how we get our clothes?"

St. Ledger dipped his head under the clear water and came up playfully, spouting water like a whale. "Of course, your clothes. If my driver did what he was told, you should find them in the dressing room. Oh, by the way, ask him to drive you home; I shan't need him for several hours."

"Oh, no, that's all right; we are too drunk to go straight home—we will walk, thank you." Emilio waved goodbye once more to the two men in the pool. Sir John, very drunk, waggled his fingers in their direction as they walked off barefoot over the Persian rugs and under the Moorish arches to the changing rooms.

Lord St.Ledger and Sir John watched them disappear. "Extraordinary fellow." The words floated across the pool to St. Ledger.

"I like him, he plays a good game of cards."

"That's true enough, though I could do without seeing too much of his fat friend."

St. Ledger spouted more water. "John, you are such a snob. Those sort of people live a real life. It took a great deal of nerve to hang on to that ticket."

Sir John splashed over in the water. "Or a great deal of stupidity."

In the changing room, a maid fussed about taking the boys' clothes from the cardboard boxes and hanging them on hangers, and a fresh bottle of champagne awaited them in an ice bucket. Bellucci, full of himself, screwed off the cork, spilling foaming wine on the floor. Emilio hoped that he wasn't as drunk as his friend, but realised that he was dressing with some difficulty.

The maid had left the room for a few minutes; when she returned, she brought with her Esmeralda and Consuela, both now dressed in different clothes than those in which they had started the evening. The girls fussed about, helping the semi-drunk Italians to dress.

Esmeralda smoothed Bellucci's hair and patted him here and there. "I hope you will come to see me again, my little friend." She adjusted his tie. "There, you look respectable. Now, you give Esmeralda her tip."

Bellucci looked at Emilio for advice. Emilio slowly patted his pockets. "Si, a tip." He went to Bellucci, stuck his hand into the fat man's money pocket, and retrieved the fifty pounds. He gave the girls twenty-five each. "You buy yourself something nice to remember us by."

Emilio looked at Bellucci, His face was a picture as he watched his bundle of fivers disappear into the girl's safe places. Both men were shown to the door and given goodnight kisses, promising to return as the maid let them out of the back door into a mews behind Jermyn Street.

The fresh air hit them like a sledgehammer. Emilio and Bellucci staggered along Piccadilly, singing snippets of Italian love songs. The Fortnum and Mason clock struck five, its clockwork figures doing their little dance in the frosty morning air. Passing the Ritz Hotel, they sang to the doorman who shooed them along.

The quickest way to Battersea was across St. James's Park to Victoria, and then along the Embankment. The gates of the park were closed; they would not be unlocked until six-thirty. Emilio helped his fat friend climb the fence, which would have been difficult enough had he been sober; but he was not sober, and the task proved difficult.

Bellucci tottered on the railing, then fell rather than jumped into the park, ripping the turn up of his trousers as he went. Emilio vaulted the fence and walked on in silence.

"What's the matter with you? Didn't you have a good time?"

Emilio shrugged. "I had a great time."

"So what's the matter?"

"Stai zitto!"

Bellucci attempted one of his happy dances, almost falling over. "I know what it is. Willi Willi Willow..."

"Shut up." Emilio walked ahead.

"You see, I'm right. Willow, she get you with that kiss." Bellucci made some kissing noises.

"Okay. Okay. It's Willow! She's a real lady; she wants me to telephone her, and she lives in Belgravia."

Bellucci ran to catch up. "Cretino! She's after your money."

"Fuck off. She fall in love with me."

"With your money, you mean."

Emilio took a clip at Bellucci's ear. missing as Bellucci staggered out of the way. Emilio chased the squealing fat man, grabbing him by the coat tails. Both men fell to the damp grass and rolled about, laughing.

Bellucci stopped laughing as suddenly as he had started. "Eh. How many times you screw Consuela?" He made a rude gesture with his fist.

"Mind your own business." Emilio clipped Bellucci's ear.

"Esmeralda, Esmeralda, four times."

"So now you are Valentino? Schifosa! Let's go home. Nazarena is going to kill me."

They climbed to their feet. Bellucci looked at Emilio's face. "She will if she see the lipstick all over your face, and you stink of scent like a puta."

Emilio rubbed his face; seeing a horse trough, he walked over to it. He took off his coat jacket and washed his face in the cold water, to the sound of Bellucci trying to sing like the great Caruso.

There was still a mob outside the café even though the station clock stood at ten past six. Emilio realised that the mob was mostly pressmen who had waited all night for their story. As they approached, flashbulbs popped, and reporters scrambled after them with questions.

"Emilio how does it feel to win the sweepstake?"

"What's the first thing you will do with your money?"

Emilio pushed through the mob and hammered on the café door.

A fresh barrage of flashbulbs lit up the street. Scippio looked through the window, then opened the door. With difficulty, Emilio and Bellucci fought their way inside and slammed the door shut. There were people crashed out everywhere. Those that were awake shook the sleepers into life. Nazarena had been dozing in a chair but awoke instinctively at the first hint of the punter's return. Scippio proudly held out his hand.

"Complimenti, Signor Scala, I heard the race on the wireless. We all did, it was incredible."

Emilio ruffled the boy's hair; next out of the crowd to greet him was his son Joe. Jumping up, he flung his arms around his father's neck. Emilio picked him up as he glanced at the potential thunderstorm brewing on Nazarena's face. "Papa, are we millionaires?"

Emilio reached in to his coat pocket and pulled out the big bar of chocolate that he had bought at Fazakerley Station. "Here, share this out with the kids." Joe pushed his way through the grown-ups, picking up a procession of children as he went.

Umberto, who had been snoring soundly, sprang as quickly as his old bones would allow into a sort of dance as he sang and played a welcome home song. Emilio shook everybody's hand as he passed through the café, getting closer and closer to the waiting Nazarena. Bellucci followed him.

Kisses, hugs, pats on the back, handshakes; finally he reached her and, ignoring her feigned protestations, picked her up in a bear hug and swung her around in time to the music, which now included the swirling sound of a piano accordion.

Emilio continued to spin his protesting wife in circles; he was home where he belonged, with his wife and kids and friends, and with the winning ticket of the Sweepstake in his pocket. Relieved now that Nazarena was not going to make a public scene, he lowered her to the floor. "Bellucci, tell those newspaper men to come in and take a picture of me and my wife and the kids. Then everybody can go home. I got a lot to do today.

# CHAPTER TWENTY-ONE

George Lloyd sat at the wheel of Toby Grant's car, which crawled over Vauxhall bridge, stuck behind a brewers dray; its four giant shire horses clip-clopped over the cobbles. Grant looked out of the car window in silence, surveying the river that twisted away like a thick silver snake. George Lloyd pulled the car out and overtook the carthorses. "We were very unlucky, Mr. Grant."

Grant kept his eyes on the river. "Unlucky? Unlucky? You think I don't know that? I had to watch the race and, on top of that, the little wop almost sold me half his ticket two minutes before the off. Now then, how much did you get on Grakle?"

Lloyd looked sheepish as he kept his eyes on the road. "Very little, Mr. Grant. We managed to get a couple of grand on with the small offices; that won us fourteen grand, but we got hit pretty hard by the punters—as you know, a lot of people backed the winner."

Grant looked angrier than he actually was. He had already done his arithmetic; at the end of the day he had just about broken even—that was, if he included the thirty grand he had taken at the card table. Although he felt like showing off, he withheld this information from his employee; best to let him squirm. "I've thrown away nearly thirty grand in cold blood. That's the last time I'll listen to one of your brilliant ideas."

George Lloyd's Adam's apple bobbed up and down as he considered how unfair his boss's last remark was. "With respect, Mr. Grant, it was Miss Rutherford's idea."

Toby Grant banged his fist onto the dashboard at the mention of Willow's name. "You approved it, okay? Now don't ever mention that woman's name to me again."

They drove on in silence along the Vauxhall embankment. Lloyd decided to get all the bad news over with. "There is one more thing, Mr. Grant."

Toby looked at his driver. "Go on."

"Snowy and Ginger got themselves pinched."

"For Christ's sake! Am I involved?"

Lloyd tried to be cheerful about the problem. "No, no. They had a bit of trouble with the Ford; we'll have to buy a new one."

"That's all I need. Where are they?"

"They're in the clink in Walsall."

Grant shook his head in disgust. "Get them out. I've got work for them."

The car drove through the back streets of Battersea in silence until it pulled up by a barbershop with a striped pole sticking out of the wall above the door. "Here we are, Mr. Grant. This is the place: DeMarco's Barbershop."

"You wait here." Grant straightened his hat, adjusted his overcoat, and climbed out of the car. He looked every bit a gangster as he crossed the pavement and entered the shop.

DeMarco was sitting on one of the barber chairs, reading a newspaper. He looked up as Grant entered.

"Mr DeMarco, rumour has it that you're very unhappy about Scala winning the Sweepstake."

DeMarco climbed out of the chair and watched Grant walk across the shop. He went to the wall where the DeMarco Sweepstake card hung and ran his finger down the list of names, stopping at the bottom.

"Toby Grant is my name; I think we can do a bit of business."

# CHAPTER TWENTY TWO

Emilio opened his eyes; his head felt as if it were full of marbles. He could hear the familiar sounds of Nazarena and the kids in the kitchen. He turned over and buried his head in the pillow, only to be roused once more by a loud knocking on the front door.

He heard Nazarena walk across the stone floor and climb the eight steps to the bedroom. The knocking on the door continued as she spoke from the bedroom doorway. "Emilio, you gotta do something. These people outside, they never stop. I not answer the door no more. All they want is for you to give them money."

Emilio rolled over in bed. At least she had stopped going on about his night out with Bellucci. He felt that he had disguised his guilt quite well, managing to be so euphoric about winning the Sweepstake that she hadn't detected any funny business.

"I'll get rid of them and lock the gates in the yard."

"I already lock the gates; this one, he climb over the top."

Emilio sat up and scratched his head. "Okay. I come down." He climbed out of bed and pulled on his trousers and a shirt, then followed his wife downstairs.

Looking through the window was the face of a scruffy young man, who on seeing some activity, continued his knocking on the door. Emilio opened it, and the man pulled off his cap. "Mr Scala! I am sorry to be bothering you, and I apologise for climbing over your wall, but I don't know where to turn. As you have won so much money, I've plucked up courage to ask you to help me."

Emilio had been hearing this for two days now; some of the stories had been amazing, and he wondered what this one was going to be. After the first day, Emilio had made a decision not to give anything to anybody, at least until he collected his prize. Even then, he would be very careful. He didn't want to be made a fool of in the community, to be considered a soft touch. He listened to the man go on about his wife and baby and rent and medicine. He studied the man's face for signs of an abject liar but couldn't find any.

He pushed a pound note into the man's hand; then, for Nazarena's sake, who was listening in the kitchen, told the man in a stern and angry voice, "I don't have any money; if I did have it, do you expect me to give it to everybody who climbs over my wall? Now get out the way you came in before I throw you out."

The man pushed the note into his pocket and backed off, replacing his cap on his head.

"Go on, away with you," Emilio said once more for good measure. He watched the young man climb over the wall, then closed the kitchen door. "That's how to deal with them. Can I have some coffee?"

Nazarena poured a kettle full of boiling water into a large zinc bathtub set on the floor in front of the stove. "Have your bath, you gonna be late for Mr. Carter; it is already eleven o'clock."

Nazarena draped a towel over a clotheshorse to shield her naked husband from the children, who played houses under the kitchen table. Emilio undressed and dipped his toe into the tub before Nazarena could warn him, "Be careful, it's hot."

She was too late; Emilio let out a curse, and Nazarena laughed out loud covering her mouth with her hand.

"Give me a kettle of cold water. Are you trying to cook me like a chicken?" He was thankful that he had seen his wife laugh; for some reason she had been miserable since he had won the Sweepstake. She fetched the water, and then while her husband bathed, she hung up his pressed suit and a clean shirt.

At exactly one o'clock, Emilio entered the offices of Weatherby and Nash in Pall Mall. He walked through the colonnaded outer door and over the flagstone floor to a middle-aged receptionist. "My name is Scala. I have an appointment with Mr. Carter."

"Yes, sir, please take a seat."

Emilio was far too nervous to sit down. He was about to pick up his Sweepstake cheque—a cheque for three hundred and fifty-seven thousand pounds. He paced about the hall, catching sight of himself in a large mirror in front of which was a flower arrangement. He took a good look at himself in the glass. Was it possible that he had changed in a couple of days? He had spent years unaware of his clothes other than, of course, that they were clean; he had never considered himself a stylish man. But now that he was about to be rich, he would take more care. He took a carnation from the flower arrangement and put it in his buttonhole, then straightened his tie. The new dark blue suit fitted well; he decided to buy a new hat in the shop that he had seen around the corner.

As he pondered the possibilities of a visit to Locks the hatter's, Carter appeared at a door. "Mr. Scala. Sorry to have kept you waiting, come in."

Emilio walked into the office, putting the hat he no longer wanted on the desk, and took the seat that Carter offered him.

"Would you like some tea?"

Emilio looked around the stark, charmless office. "No thank you. You said on the telephone that I would not have to go to Dublin for my money."

Carter twiddled a pencil, not wanting to catch Emilio's eye. "That's correct. However, there is a problem."

Emilio felt a hammer blow in his chest; a cold sweat broke out on his forehead, and he could hear his own blood pumping through his veins. He struggled to pull himself together, thankful that Carter was not looking at him. Taking in a deep breath, he sighed silently. "Problem. What problem?"

Carter looked up from his desk; this man had delivered bad news as a profession for many years, and it never got any easier. "The Irish Sweep Trust have received an injunction requesting them to withhold payment to you pending the outcome of a court hearing, regarding a claim by a syndicate headed by a Mr. DeMarco to a major share in your ticket. And I must tell you that the request has been sanctioned by the Irish court."

Emilio could sit no longer; he stood up and paced the office. "What does all this mean? Injunction?"

Carter picked up a pair of spectacles and began polishing them with a handkerchief. "It means, Mr. Scala, that the court feels that this Mr. DeMarco has sufficient evidence to his claim to justify a court hearing. The money will be held by the Sweepstake Trust until a decision by the court is made."

Emilio punched his right fist into his left palm. Almost speechless with rage, he snatched up his hat from the desk. He then pulled the ticket from his waistcoat pocket. "This is crazy. Look, this is my ticket. It's my ticket. I won the Sweepstake. DeMarco is a fucking liar."

Carter watched Emilio apprehensively; he was getting volatile. "Calm down, Mr. Scala. I'm sure everything will work out. But you are going to need some help."

Emilio leant on the desk in a threatening manner. "Look, I don't need any help. This ticket is mine."

Carter, the professional that he was, continued to try to make Emilio get the picture. "Quite so, Mr. Scala, but you are going to need a lawyer. I can't help you personally, as I am retained by the Sweepstake Trust, but I'd be pleased to recommend somebody."

Emilio had had enough of this; all he wanted to do at this minute was to strangle DeMarco and any other lying bastard in the syndicate. "Thank you, Mr. Carter. I will be in touch with you."

Emilio turned and walked out the door through the reception hall and into the street, oblivious to the passing crowd; his face set in a furious mask he strode off along the wide pavements of Pall Mall.

The pub where Emilio took refuge was in a mews behind Jermyn Street. By coincidence, it was close to the scene of his bawdy night out with Bellucci and the toffs. The fact did nothing to help him clear his mind. He ordered a pint of Bass with a whisky chaser on the side and took it to an alcove table, where he hoped he could sit and think out his problems. When he had left his house, his day had been planned. Such a perfect day, whistling down the street in his best suit, en route to pick up a millionaire's cheque. He was to have entered the restaurant to meet Willow for lunch, rich and full of confidence. He had even promised himself a new hat.

Now as he sipped his whisky, he had no cheque, no new hat, and certainly not enough confidence to have lunch with the fabulous Willow. Was Bellucci right? Was he making a fool of himself? Was Willow only interested in his Sweepstake prize? Was he just a foolish man cheating on a wonderful, caring, and practical wife, just to be taken for a ride by a cunning and ruthless social beauty? And that bastard DeMarco, the lying stronzo. He would deal with him later.

In the meantime, what did a man do whose world suddenly fell to pieces? He knocked back the scotch. 'Is it possible that the good Lord thinks so little of me that he would torture me like this? Why would he give such good fortune with one hand and take it away with the other?' Emilio drank the beer. 'He is testing me. I will fight this thing; I will take my prize. Fuck DeMarco. And Willow—I will find her out.'

Emilio looked at the pub clock. It was ten to two. He went into the gents, took a piss, combed his hair, and put his hat on. He noticed that it had a small hole where the front crease had been worn out from at least three years of wear. 'Fuck it, I shall buy a new hat anyway.'

Emilio left the pub. En route to his lunch appointment, he stopped at Locks and bought himself a fine new hat. The hat seemed to refresh his spirits. On entering the Ritz hotel, he had already decided—for the time being, at least—to put his problems aside. He left his new hat with the cloakroom attendant, carefully pocketing the ticket. Unable to resist the elaborate men's room, he went in for a final spruce up. Satisfied, he wandered the hotel until he found the restaurant.

Controlling a fresh wave of insecurity, Emilio approached the Maitre d'Hôtel. "Good afternoon, sir. Can I help you?"

Emilio looked around the palm- and screen-decorated room, hoping to find the friendly face of Willow among the sea of smart diners. "Miss Rutherford has reserved a table for lunch."

"Ah. yes. You must be Signor Scala. Please follow me."

Emilio, relieved that something had gone right, followed the Maitre d'Hôtel through the crowded room to a discreet window table, taking the seat where he could watch the door. He ordered a whisky soda and settled down to wait.

Fifteen minutes later, Willow made her entrance. As usual, she looked stunning in a red and white striped two-piece woollen suit of dress and jacket; the brim of her red hat was broader than any other in the room. Emilio watched the heads turn as the Maitre d'Hôtel guided Willow through the tables. He watched her stop here and there to chat briefly to the odd acquaintance, wiping his palms discreetly on his trousers as she approached. The Maitre d'Hotel pulled out her chair, and Willow swished into it as Emilio stood up. "Emilio. Sorry I'm late; I hope you haven't been too bored."

Emilio sat down and looked at the relaxed vision before him. She was so soft and smooth; he caught a faint hint of her perfume, and his spine tingled. "Would you like to drink something?"

"Champagne, please—anything else makes me cry." Willow turned to the hovering Maitre d'Hôtel. "A bottle of my usual, please, Gaston." As the waiter departed, she turned back to Emilio. "You will help me drink it, won't you?"

"Anything to stop you from crying. I can't imagine you crying."

Willow made a fragile, feminine face. "I very nearly did at the races, when you refused to sell Toby Grant part of your ticket."

"Was it that important to you?"

"At the time, yes, it was."

Emilio took a slug of his whisky. "I very nearly did. Sell it, I mean. Your eyes dared me not to."

Willow looked surprised at Emilio's last remark, realising that she had done something wrong at the races. "Is that what you thought?"

Emilio looked into her eyes. "Didn't you?"

Willow looked away rather than answer the question. Emilio returned to the subject of crying. "You are so beautiful and confident—what could you have to cry about?"

A waiter arrived with the champagne and filled the glasses.

"You would be surprised, Emilio."

"I'm sure you have everything. You have men falling at your feet."

Willow took a sip from her glass. "Most of the men I meet are children. But to watch a man dice with fate on the scale as you did... I think that was the most daring thing that I have ever seen a man do."

Emilio fiddled with his wedding ring. "Are you saying that you like me?"

Willow gave Emilio her most expansive smile. "Are you crazy? I'm mad about you."

Emilio noticed that Willow had laid her hand on the table; a diamond ring sparkled on her middle finger. The pale hand looked fragile and lonely, so he put his on top of it and squeezed. "So what you got to cry about?"

Willow left her hand where it was, apparently enjoying the contact of Emilio's strong fingers. "You being married, for one thing."

Emilio squeezed her hand. "What's that to you?"

Willow took her hand away. "It means that I can't have you."

"Does it?"

Willow gave Emilio a long, enquiring smile. "Doesn't it?"

An hour later in a much emptier restaurant, Willow and Emilio ate strawberries as the waiter poured the last glasses from the second bottle of Champagne.

"I'm going on a grand tour of Italy. Venice, Capri; you could come with me," she said provocatively.

"If only I could. I would love that. I hardly know Italy. I left my village Isola when I was fourteen. I ran away to Rome with the circus."

Willow looked genuinely interested. "Did you?"

Emilio, loose-tongued from the wine, had no trouble continuing his story. "I was an acrobat. I was famous with the tourists. I could walk up the Spanish Steps on my hands, my cap hanging from my mouth to collect the pennies as I went up and down."

Willow laughed at the thought. "You must show me that trick sometime."

Emilio drained his glass and beamed a huge white-toothed smile. "I will show you now, if you like."

Willow reached across the table and took Emilio's hand. "Not here, for heaven's sake; take me home."

Emilio put his arm through Willow's and led her down the steps of the Ritz into the vaulted arcade that covered the pavement. Emilio hailed the first taxi at the rank. A photographer stepped forward and took a picture, catching Emilio completely by surprise.

Willow pushed Emilio towards the taxi. "Get in the cab; I'll deal with him."

For some reason, Emilio did what he was told. He watched from the window as Willow approached the photographer and talked to him. He saw her open her bag and give the man something; turning away, she hurried back to the taxi and climbed in. She gave the driver her Belgrave Square address and settled back into her seat, hoping that her friend Billy Brown the photographer would get the picture published in tonight's edition of the Standard. This was not, however, what she told Emilio.

"That should be all right. I bought him off; he would only get a couple of pounds from a picture editor, so I gave him a fiver."

Emilio looked worried. "Can you trust those fellows?"

Willow took Emilio's hand. "Not a hundred percent."

"My wife must not see that picture."

"Don't worry, Emilio, it will be all right."

Emilio was feeling too good to let the situation worry him for long; he had consumed several whiskies and at least one bottle of champagne. And with the sweet-smelling Willow snuggling up to him in the back of the cab, he could think of nothing else but the possibility of getting her into bed.

Emilio could not believe how quickly it had happened; they drank a bottle of champagne and talked for a bit and laughed a lot. He remembered walking on his hands round and round her bed, and then he was in it with her wearing nothing but a silk robe and him in his underpants, and she tearing at him and moaning and kissing him in places that he had never been kissed, and he stroking her smooth young body and kissing her in places that he had never dared kiss his wife. They made love in a frantic semi-drunken state, and he had spun on the bed, his head going round and round with this beauty on top of him and underneath him.

They rolled across the floor, locked together. When they finally stopped, he found himself panting and out of breath, his knees stinging from the friction of the carpet. He was entwined with her on the floor, in the corner of her bedroom, uncomfortably crammed against the hard, sharp leg of an upturned coffee table. He lay there, catching his breath, the beautiful Willow in his arms. Her eyes were closed, short gasps of warm breath coming from her parted lips.

Now for DeMarco, the son of a bitch.

# CHAPTER TWENTY THREE

Emilio walked with a spring in his step from Battersea station. He left by the side entrance to avoid the possibility of being spotted by Nazarena or anyone else from the café, skirting the water bottling factory, passing Jimmy the news vendor.

"Hey, Lucky! She's a cracker."

Emilio waved, not fully taking in the remark. He took a left onto Bellucci's street and made directly for the fat man's house. Emilio knocked urgently on the window. There was no reply. He tried the door and it opened. Calling out to Bellucci, there was still no reply, so he ran up the short staircase and looked into Bellucci's bedroom, but a shabby wardrobe and an unmade bed was all he found. Impatiently, he ran back down the stairs and onto the street as the gasman cycled by with his lamp-lighting pole and lit the light in the lamppost. Emilio walked past him with a nod of recognition in the direction of DeMarco's barbershop, which took just a few minutes.

Emilio's adrenalin was pumping—what, with the champagne, the excitement of a couple of hours in Willow's bed, and the anger at DeMarco's fucking lies. He arrived at the barber's like a bull, but the shop was closed and the blinds drawn. Emilio could hear voices coming from within; he tried the door, but it was locked, so he gave it a savage kick just below the lock, and it sprang open with a crash.

DeMarco was sitting, reading a newspaper; two other men that Emilio did not know stood by the wall, but he ignored them.

"DeMarco, stronzo, have you gone fucking mad, you lying bastard?"

DeMarco jumped from his chair instinctively and stood behind it for security. Emilio walked right through the chair and grabbed at the barber, who twisted out of the way, waving the newspaper. "It's you who have gone crazy; suddenly you are a big shot. You spend our money on putans. Look at this, you schifosa"

Emilio didn't have to look too hard. The front page carried a large photo of himself and Willow leaving the Ritz. The headline read, 'LUCKY EMILIO, PUTTING ON THE RITZ while court stops Sweepstake payment.'

"You greedy bastard. This is just the beginning; you gonna share this prize with me and the boys."

"Vaffanculo, I will. I'll see you in your grave first." Emilio tried once more to get at the barber, when Ginger came swiftly up behind him and gave him one smart crack across the back of the head with a black jack. Emilio crumpled into a heap at his feet.

DeMarco came out from behind his fallen chair. "I told you he was a stubborn fellow."

Ginger turned Emilio over with his foot. "Don't worry about that; we'll soften him up. He'll be as good as gold by the time we finish with him. Snowy, get the car."

DeMarco watched nervously as Ginger picked Emilio up and slung him fireman fashion over his shoulder. Ginger waited until Snowy brought a car to the front of the shop, then looked to see that the coast was clear before bundling Emilio into the back seat.

The car drove away, leaving a shaken DeMarco at the door of his shop. Ginger sat in the back with the unconscious Emilio. "Drive him to Noddy's warehouse; we can deal with him there."

Snowy drove the car over the river to Chelsea wharf, where he turned into the green gates of a semi-derelict brick warehouse with a tin and glass roof. Here and there, great white patches of pigeon shit adorned packing cases and the concrete floor. He parked the car next to a flatbed truck. The place was stacked with old crates, barrels, bits of building machinery and all manner of rubbish.

In one corner was a camp bed; a dirty old eider down cover lay across it. Ginger carried Emilio from the car, pulled off his clothes, and dumped him unceremoniously into a large barrel, then took the eider down from the camp bed to the barrel. He took a knife from his pocket and ripped the thing to shreds, making sure that the billowing clumps of feathers fell into the barrel.

In the meantime, Snowy busied himself with what looked like a watering can, the kind used to pour hot pitch into cracks in the road. Taking it to a large tar barrel, he turned the tap; very slowly, a thick black treacly substance dripped from the tap. After a few seconds, the flow improved until it poured thickly into the can. When it was quite full, snowy took it over to the barrel and poured it over the unconscious Emilio's head. He repeated this process several times until Ginger stopped him, then threw Emilio's clothes into the barrel.

"That will do—now bang that lid on." Snowy did as he was told. The two men heaved the barrel on to its side and began to playfully roll it about the warehouse.

"I'm gonna pour one more can full through the bung ole, that should coat him." Ginger took the bung from the side of the barrel while Snowy poured. "Hold it steady; we don't want to make a mess, now do we?"

Both men laughed as Ginger banged back the bung. They rolled the barrel over to the flatbed truck and, using two planks for a ramp, rolled the barrel onto it. They stood the barrel up and removed the lid. "We don't want him brown bread, do we?"

Snowy laughed, phlegm gurgling in his consumptive chest. "Black bread, more like." His chest rattled again as he chuckled at his own joke.

"Right then, we better deliver him."

The black sticky mass in the barrel moved and groaned as the lorry pulled out of the warehouse gates.

Bellucci had tried in vain to explain away the picture in the newspaper. Nazarena had completely blown her top when she had seen it—courtesy of little Jimmy the news vendor. At one point she had got so bad that Bellucci and Scippio had closed the café and pulled the curtains so that they could try and calm her down in privacy. She had eventually subsided into a miserable sobbing state, presumably to conserve her energy for row she intended to have upon Emilio's return.

Bellucci tried to get through the sobs once more. "It's not true. He must have been doing some business; she is a business woman, I know her."

Nazarena snatched open the newspaper and spread it on the table, giving the picture a smack with the flat of her hand. "It is true. It's black and a white. I've seen him carrying on, with her silk stockings and automobiles. He's wicked. That's what he is. Wicked."

Furiously calm, Nazarena picked up a kitchen knife in her frustration. "If he comes home, I kill him, I stick this knife through him, and you see if I don't."

Bellucci put his face in his hands for inspiration. A screech of brakes outside in the street stopped the argument; there was something urgent about the noise. Scippio went to the window in time to see a barrel being rolled off the back of a lorry, unable to do anything as it burst on impact with the cobblestones. He stood frozen as the lorry sped away.

Bellucci was the first out the door. Amongst the broken wood, there stirred a sticky black groaning apparition. The next thing Bellucci was aware of was Nazarena's scream, it shattered the night silence. "Scippio get her inside; I will bring him in. Subito."

Bellucci attempted to pick the sticky mess up off the road but couldn't do it. Bending down, he tried to scrape the muck from Emilio's face, clogging his own hands with tar and feathers. "Bastards, porco Dio! Emilio, are you alright under all this shit?"

Emilio groaned and coughed; his mouth was full of the stuff. With his finger, Bellucci cleared the mouth; then with the tails of his shirt, he wiped Emilio's face the best he could. Emilio choked and tried to spit. "Get this shit off... it stinks like a goat's arse."

Bellucci made a sign of the cross. "I get you inside, then we clean you up."

Nazarena could be restrained no longer and came running back out. With a blanket, they wrapped Emilio and dragged him inside.

"Have you got petrol?" Bellucci asked as he carried him inside.

Nazarena had now switched to the strong protective wife mode, forgetting for the time being that she was about to murder her man.

Scippio came back from the yard with petrol and rags. Nazarena lifted Emilio's head. "Don't speak. You lie still; we soon clean you up."

At first, Bellucci tried to be a bit fastidious about cleaning the mess of his friend, but as this didn't work, a more drastic approach was called for. He carefully peeled off the congealed remnants of Emilio's best suit; it came away in an awkward-looking lump, jacket and trousers mashed together in thick black toffee tar. "Scissors, get me some scissors."

He cut off Emilio's underpants and peeled off the socks, revealing extremely white feet and genitals. "At least I haven't got to scrub your balls." Bellucci chuckled at his own joke, trying to make light of the situation.

Nazarena started wiping Emilio down with a petrol-soaked rag as Bellucci tried to deal with his head. "I'm going to have to take your hair off." He lifted an arm the armpit was clogged with tar. "And shave your arm pits. How you feel?"

"Just get this shit off me, the fucking petrol stings."

Bellucci snipped with gummed-up scissors at Emilio's hair, and it came away in chunks. "This is no good. Help me drag him into the yard; we need buckets of soapy water, and turpentine."

A couple of hours later, Emilio sat in front of the blazing stove in the cottage, wrapped in blankets with a steaming mug of coffee. His head was shaved and covered in red marks where the tar had been rubbed off, and a blue ridge ran down the back of his skull just behind his right ear. Apart from the soreness resulting from superficial petrol irritation, he was physically unscathed.

Bellucci warmed his hands in the glow. "With that haircut you look like Mussolini."

"Vaffanculo!"

Emilio turned to Nazarena, not knowing that she was hovering on the verge of a volcanic attack at his infidelity. "Nazarena, scusi, I want to talk to Bellucci."

Nazarena finally cracked. "You wanna talk. You talk to me. 'cause I'm gonna kill you."

She whopped him around the head with the offending newspaper and as if from nowhere produced her carving knife, brandishing it with no real hint of danger in front of his face. Emilio buried his head in his hands, partly to defend himself but more specifically to think of a way out of this situation. Nazarena gave him one more whack with the newspaper; then, throwing them down, she ran sobbing into the night.

The kids woke up; two of them crept cautiously down the stairs to find their father sitting despondently with his shaven head in his hands, wrapped in a blanket. Bellucci shooed them back up stairs. "Back to bed; I come up to see you in a minute."

The kids did as they were told.

"Emilio, don't worry, you are the luckiest man in the world. You will get out of trouble."

Emilio looked at Bellucci through the cracks in his fingers. "Bellucci, fetch the grappa."

Nazarena pulled her shawl about her, using a damp corner of it to wipe her tear-stained face. She had never walked these streets at this time of night, even though she had lived here for years. The gaslights lit up yellow circles on the pavements under the lamps. Only the cats stirred; a dustbin lid clattered to the cobbles in an alleyway, frightening her. The dark shadowy doorways also frightened her. She moved to the centre of the road.

Gambling was the cause of all this trouble. She asked God why she had been cursed with a gambler for a husband. God did not reply.

She could take the kids to her cousin's cousin in Skegness. She could teach him a lesson and use her secret savings to take her family home to Italy. She could give him one more chance, but how could she forgive him for making such a poppy show of himself and her with that putan in the newspapers? Then she thought about Emilio covered in tar and laying in the road like a dog. What unspeakable trouble was he in for people to do that to him? He was a good man, but the bastard gambling was the ruin of him, of all the family. She wished that he had lost everything; at least he would have to be at home.

She would work, and by working would feel secure. Holding the family together was what she was good at. All this money spoilt everything; there was no control.

She turned a corner, hoping to double back in the direction of the railway bridge. She prayed to God for a sign that everything would be all right. As if in answer to her prayer, she heard her name called on the night air. The street that she was in was dark; it only had one lamp, and that she had left behind on the corner. Again she heard her name.

Out of the shadows appeared Emilio, riding his tricycle. She stood there, petrified, until she recognised him. Her immediate reaction was to run away, but she could not move. Emilio climbed off the bike and picked her up; effortlessly, he sat her on the box of the tricycle. She didn't resist, just pulled her shawl around her face while he climbed back on and in silence peddled her back to the café.

Emilio carefully shaved his head, running the razor in short sweeps from his forehead to the nape of his neck. It had been three days since the tarring and feathering, and the bruise on the back of his head had turned into a grey smudge. Nazarena had taken the news that he might not get his prize money with remarkable restraint; he felt that she had almost been pleased. He wiped his head with a towel. Nazarena paused from ironing a white shirt to put a hot coal from the stove into the heavy iron.

"Where is my clean shirt?" Emilio groped about with one hand while towelling his head with the other.

"Ask that fancy woman—you see if she can iron your shirts. If you see her again I won't be here when you come back."

Emilio pulled the towel from his head. "Come on, now," he said nicely. "That was business. I told you, she is a friend of St. Ledger. He is going to help me. Where is my shirt?"

"Basta! Ferma. Sei pieno di merda. You are still lying to me, so stop. I forgive you this once. She is very beautiful. Stai zito, finish, that is it. NO More. Or it will be the last time." Nazarena threw the shirt at him. She was not a happy woman.

She went to a drawer and took out a tie, putting it on the table next to an open cardboard box, from which the now-shirted Emilio took out a new suit. He dressed in silence as his wife continued her ironing. Satisfied, he looked in the kitchen mirror. Nazarena looked away in disgust. He picked up a brush and tried to brush himself down. Nazarena put down the iron and forcefully took away the brush; she then did the job herself, straightening his tie for good measure.

Emilio heard the car drive into the yard. "Here's the car. How do I look?"

"Like a bastard. I mean it. Next time I take the kids and we go home to Isola."

Emilio gave her a hug to pacify her. "It's all right. I got a lot of business; she don't mean nothing."

Emilio gave his wife a kiss on the cheek and let himself out. He walked across the yard, the only sign of his recent ordeal his shaved head, which in fact suited him. He put on his hat as he approached Lord St. Ledger's limousine, which was parked just out of sight of the cottage. The chauffeur opened the door. Sitting in the back seat was Willow, her long legs crossed, tapered into shapely silk clad ankles that ended in a pair of beige snakeskin shoes. "Bunkie sent me to fetch you; I hope you don't mind?"

Emilio, a little surprised, turned to see if there was any possibility of Nazarena seeing the occupant of the car. Believing he was safe, he quickly climbed in, and the limousine pulled away.

In an upstairs window Nazarena let the curtain that she peeped through drop.

"I'm terribly sorry about the newspaper, I hope it didn't cause you too much trouble." Willow sounded genuinely concerned.

The limousine crossed Battersea Bridge. Emilio watched a long line of barges cut through the silver sheet of water below. "Trouble! Life is trouble; at the moment I have plenty trouble."

Willow put her hand on his. "That's why I came today. I had no other way of getting in touch with you. I hope you don't mind. I just wanted to apologise for allowing us to be so indiscreet. It was my fault, taking you to the Ritz. I should have known better."

Emilio looked at the beautiful face, wanting to believe her sincerity. "Nonsense! I'm a big boy, I catch my own trouble. It's not your fault."

Willow gave Emilio a curious look. "There's something different about you, Emilio! What is it?" She was looking at the side of his face. He lifted his hat and smiled. "Good God! What have you done?"

Emilio replaced his hat. "It's a long story."

Willow leaned across and took of the hat, running her hand over his bald head. "You look like a gladiator, how exciting."

Emilio took back his hat and put it on, not sure if she was kidding him.

They continued the short journey in silence, until the limousine pulled into the drive of a large white Victorian house in the Boltons. Stone lions stood guard on the entrance lintels. The chauffeur stopped the car at the foot of a wide flight of steps that led up to a huge door, the lapis-coloured paintwork shining as brightly as the elaborate brass knocker and keyholes. They were shown in by Bartlett the butler, who took them directly to St. Ledger's study.

They entered a tall room lit by a brass and crystal chandelier that hung from a large plaster rosette in the centre of the ceiling, and by the blaze from logs burning in the gunmetal grate of a tall marble fireplace. An oak table ran along one wall, its carved legs braced like a bulldogs, taking the weight of the trophies. Silver and gold cups littered the table. In a bowed window was the card table, even more beautiful than the one on the Pullman.

Bartlett opened a bottle of champagne and poured two glasses. "Please make yourselves comfortable. His Lordship will be down shortly."

Emilio took his drink and walked about the study. Bookcases lined with leather-bound volumes of sporting books climbed in rows to the ceiling. He read the inscriptions on the trophies. The Oaks 1927. The Derby 1921. A crystal vase was inscribed The Liverpool Cup for Coursing Greyhounds, 1927. Silver-framed photographs of horses and greyhounds stood here and there.

Willow had seen all this before and took her drink to a cushioned curved seat that ran around the window. "He lives for his sport."

"I can see." Emilio picked up a photo of St. Ledger with two boxers, about to study it when the door opened and in strode the imposing figure of Lord St. Ledger. The light from the chandelier twinkled on the silk lapels of his brocade smoking jacket and the gold embroidery on his black velvet slippers.

"Emilio! My dear fellow. Sorry to have kept you." He looked around the room, spying Willow reclining in the bay window seat. "There you are, my dear, have you got a drink?" St.Ledger went to Emilio and shook his hand; he then went to the fireplace and threw two logs on the roaring fire. "Do you play gin rummy?"

Emilio smiled, "I love to play gin rummy. Si. It's a clever game."

"Good, we shall play as we talk." St. Ledger guided Emilio to the card table, sat down, broke the seals on two decks of cards, and began shuffling them together. "Emilio, about your problem. This morning I spoke to a lawyer. He is the very best for this sort of case." St. Ledger dealt the cards while Willow relaxed, reading the current Vanity Fair.

"Will he help me?" Emilio asked, picking up his cards.

"I'm sure he will; I'll take you to meet him. He might advise you to settle."

Willow looked across from her magazine to watch Emilio's reaction to St. Ledger's last remark.

"Settling is no good to me. I owe the bookmaker fifteen grand."

St. Ledger picked up a card from the pack on the table and slid it in to the rest of his hand. "Yes, that is rather unfortunate."

He threw away the king of spades. Emilio picked it up. "Anyway, they are screwing me. I won the Sweepstake fair and square. We are going to fight this, aren't we, Bunkie?"

St. Ledger ignored Emilio's discarded seven of hearts and took another dark card from the deck. "Of course."

Emilio took another dark card. "You are a very good man for a big shot. Thank you very much."

St. Ledger laughed at Emilio's turn of phrase, as he took another card.

# CHAPTER TWENTY FOUR

Gaston Sellinger gave the impression of a bird of prey as he walked around his large carved desk. Emilio and St. Ledger sat in comfortable chairs facing him. "I'm afraid this isn't going to work." He gave Emilio a grave look over his gold-rimmed spectacles.

"No work?" was all a stunned Emilio could say. Realising this was not enough he tried again,"But Lord St. Ledger, he say he will pay."

"I can't take this case. I'm sorry." The hawkish lawyer came once more around his desk. "Payment is not the point. I'm afraid I must advise you that this case cannot be won. You must settle."

"Why?" pleaded a desperate Emilio.

"There are ten witnesses against you. It's your word against theirs."

Emilio stood up, trying desperately hard to conceal his disappointment. "Thank you very much, Mr. Sellinger I appreciate your frankness. We will go to another lawyer."

Sellinger sat on the corner of his desk, obviously annoyed that his good council had not been taken; his head jerked back as he focused on Emilio through the high polish of his gold-rimmed lenses. "That will be expensive, Mr. Scala."

Emilio looked at St. Ledger for support. "Lord St. Ledger, he will pay."

St. Ledger shifted in his seat as he caught a glance from the lawyer. "Um...Well...I'm not sure that I can."

Emilio turned on his so-called friend, a frown of disappointment on his face. "But you said..."

St. Ledger raised a hand. "I know. But a lawsuit is very expensive. And if we can't win...after all, there's no point throwing good money after bad, is there?"

Emilio, exasperated and disappointed, put on his hat. He didn't want to be rude to these important people, but the lawyer was talking rubbish, and St. Ledger agreed with him. "You said that you would help me fight this, you promised. Now you ask me to lie down, just because people want to lie against me."

St. Ledger sat looking embarrassed, twiddling the ring on his little finger. The lawyer stood up. "Mr. Scala, take my advice and settle. In cases like this it is very often the only way of achieving anything positive."

St.Ledger stopped twiddling his ring and stood up, putting his hand reassuringly on Emilio's shoulder. "Look, Emilio. I said I would help you, and I will, But I must take this sort of legal advice seriously. Mr. Sellinger is very experienced in these matters; we would be foolish to ignore what he has to say."

Emilio thought for a moment, lines of worry etched his brow. "I will go to Ireland and speak the truth for myself. I tell the truth. In the court they will believe me."

Sellinger took off his spectacles and gave them a polish with a silk handkerchief. "Unless you can get yourself some proof, I'm afraid ten witnesses will destroy you. All I can say is that if you do decide to go it alone, I will appoint one of our clerks to help you with the formalities."

Sellinger pulled a gold watch from his breast pocket and looked at the time—his signal that the meeting was over. "You will let me know what you decide to do, won't you? Now, if you would excuse me, I have some business to discuss with His Lordship."

Emilio realised that it was time for him to leave. He thanked St. Ledger with a firm handshake and left the two men to discuss their business. He walked out of the office feeling terribly alone; his whole world seemed to be falling apart. He was being robbed and felt so helpless. What could he do? The first thing was to talk to DeMarco; maybe there was a deal to be made, and maybe he should give them something, after all.

At the corner of Knightsbridge and Sloan Street, he hailed a cab.

DeMarco stirred the shaving brush in a china mug and expertly applied the white creamy foam to his customer's face. Taking a cutthroat razor from the top pocket of his white coat, he flipped it open with his thumb and deftly stropped it on a worn leather strap. He looked up at the sound of the bell that hung above the door. Emilio entered, looking drawn. DeMarco froze, holding the razor.

"You can put that away, DeMarco. I've been thinking."

DeMarco tentatively lowered the razor. He was not quite sure if Emilio was in a hostile mood. He had not seen him since Mr. Grant's men had taken him away.

"Perhaps we can reach some agreement?"


Relieved, DeMarco smiled at the prospect of this negotiation. "Emilio, listen, I'm sorry what they did. Sit down, I be with you in a moment."

Emilio sat in one of the chairs. He didn't want to discuss anything in front of DeMarco's customer. What he wanted to do was shave the fucking barber's head. He watched the razor scrape, scrape, scrape the beard from the customer's stretched-back chin. He noticed DeMarco's watch hanging on the wall and wanted to look at it. Getting up, he walked over to where it hung and took it off the nail, shook it, then held it to his ear.

DeMarco wondered what Emilio was doing; he tried to make light of the situation, waving the razor in the air. "Bloody thing, it stops again."

Emilio had an idea. He flipped open the back of the watch, looked at it, then closed it again, hanging it back on the nail next to the sweepstake card. Emilio walked casually to the door of the shop. He turned to DeMarco. "I can't make a deal with you; you are a thief. I'm going to fight you. Not with this." He smacked his fist with a crack into the palm of his hand. "With this" He tapped his bald head. "Not a penny. Not one penny you get. I got the truth. Believe me, I'm gonna squash you."

DeMarco froze with the razor, about to scrape his nervous customer's top lip.

Emilio took a couple of strides towards the barber chair and lowered his head. "You see this haircut your boys give me? Well, you better remember it. It's gonna haunt you."

Emilio left the shop, slamming the door behind him; the bell bounced uncontrollably on its spring as DeMarco's shaky razor drew a speck of blood from his customer's top lip.

Emilio's mind was racing; he hailed the first cab he saw. It took him back to Gaston Sellinger's office. Sellinger made him wait. Emilio paced up and down the carpeted corridor. The receptionist, who had been about to leave when Emilio had made his unscheduled appearance, took off her hat and coat, obviously furious. It was five past six; Mr Sellinger never took an appointment after six.

Emilio asked to use the telephone. The secretary dialled Willow's number for him. "Please pick up the black telephone, Mr Scala, your party is on the line."

It was Willow's French maid Monique that Emilio spoke to. "Can I speak to Miss Rutherford?"

"I am very sorry, she is not at home."

"It's Mr. Scala here. Did you tell her that I had called?"

"Yes, I did, Mr. Scala. Shall I give her another message?"

"Just tell her that I called again. Thank you." Emilio hung up as Sellinger came into the reception area with his last client of the day. Emilio watched the birdlike man bid a fat woman in a huge fur collared coat goodbye; she seemed to roll out of the office like a fat sheep.

Sellinger came over to Emilio. "Mr. Scala, you will find it much more convenient for yourself and me if you telephone for an appointment rather than coming to my office without warning."

Emilio looked suitably apologetic. He understood the mild reprimand. "I'm sorry, I come on the moment."

Sellinger actually smiled at Emilio's attempt to articulate his apology. "Come on in. It's past office hours. Have a drink."

Sellinger went to a cabinet that matched his elaborately carved desk.

"Whisky?" Emilio nodded. Sellinger poured the amber liquid from a decanter into squat fat crystal tumblers. He handed one to Emilio. "Help yourself to soda or water. Now then, are you having second thoughts?"

Emilio sipped his whisky neat. "No. No. I want to defend myself. I don't wanna be no trouble to no one. Except I don't know what I have to do in the court. And you said you will give me your clerk to help me."

The birdlike lawyer seemed to be a completely different person to the man Emilio had met earlier in the day. Emilio thought it was perhaps that he was no longer trying to impress His Lordship, or perhaps it was the whisky. "His Lordship is prepared to help you defend yourself. He feels it is the least he can do. He is a very sensible man and promised to help, but he felt it necessary to heed my advice. So you want to defend yourself?"

Emilio took another sip of the smooth whisky. "Yes, I do."

"Very well. I will give you the services of Mr. Slocombe, one of my clerks. He will help you with the formalities of the court. I can only wish you the very best of luck. If you will come here tomorrow at nine, I will introduce you and you can discuss the case with him. I will then give him leave to accompany you to Dublin." The lawyer drained his glass. "Will that do?"

Emilio drained his glass. "Thank you very much. You see, I win this case."

The lawyer smiled a knowing smile. "Perhaps you will."

Sellinger took his hat and coat from a closet and walked Emilio out of the office. On the pavement, he raised his hat and climbed into his waiting car. Emilio thanked the lawyer once more and walked off; passing Harvey Nichols, he turned on to Sloane Street and made his way to Belgravia.

Emilio stood for several minutes on the pavement outside Willow's flat. He made to walk away, changed his mind, walked up the steps, and rang the bell.

Willow opened it herself, obviously expecting someone else. She looked ravishing in a full-length evening dress, diamonds sparkling in her ears. "Emilio... What a surprise. You will have to excuse me—I'm in such a rush."

Emilio didn't wait for an invitation. He entered the house. "I've been calling you all afternoon. I have such problems, I had to see you.

Willow was getting impatient; she was also being rather cool. "Can it wait? I'm in a terrible hurry."

"I have to go to Dublin in a few days and I won't get a chance to see you."

"Look, why don't you call me when you get back?"

"You look beautiful, Willow."

She acknowledged the compliment with the faintest of smiles. "Look, I'm sorry, I really must rush."

Emilio got the picture; this was the big brush off. Fucking Bellucci, he was right; now he had no money he had no Willow. "Okay. I go. I thought you liked me."

"I do, Emilio, but I am a busy girl."

Emilio looked into her eyes for a few moments; then he turned and walked out the door. Willow held it open until he passed. "I'm sorry.

Emilio turned to look at her once more. "Another time. Ciao, Bella."

He walked off down the street, the words, "Good luck," followed by the sound of Willow's closing door, echoing in. his ears.

Emilio walked the broad Belgravia streets, warm light from the big-windowed houses bathing the pavements as he passed. Expensive curtains were tantalisingly drawn to reveal glimpses of a rich, secure way of life that he was so close to, yet so far from attaining. He had been reckless. Reckless with Willow; that was stupid—he wondered if Nazarena had seen Willow in the car? He would know soon enough. He took a breath that made him shudder. "Start again. Draw a line and start again."

He walked home, trying to evaluate his position. In the bank there was fifteen hundred pounds, the remains of his original winnings. He would need all of that if he were to take Mr. Slocombe to Dublin, and he would have to take Bellucci; he would need his friend during an ordeal like a court case. He had told Sellinger that he would defend himself, another reckless decision. He knew fuck all about court cases and law. The bastard DeMarco probably had some clever lawyer who was trained to hang, draw, and quarter innocent men. If he lost the case, he would be broke again, and humiliated—not to mention the rage that would grow and gnaw at his soul. He was not a man who could lie down after being cheated. What would he do? He would murder DeMarco, that's what he would do.

Emilio walked across the gas-lit Battersea Bridge. In the midst of his confusion, he knew one clear thing. They would not cheat him easily; they would not cheat him without the mother of all fights. Tomorrow he would sit down with this Mr. Slocombe and deliver his plan. As he continued his walk home, he prayed that his wife and kids would still be there.

Seagulls swooped and turned in the wind that cracked the flying pendants that decorating the passenger deck at the stern of the steamship Dublin Castle as it cut a wide, foaming wake through the

Irish Sea. Emilio, Bellucci, and Slocombe sat discussing the case. They had retreated to a cabin to escape the attentions of the curious crowd on the passenger deck. As a result of massive press coverage of the impending case, Emilio had rapidly become a household celebrity. No one had ever won so much money. And the fact that he might lose it all in an Irish court had stimulated Fleet Street in to a frenzy of speculation.

The Dublin Castle was crammed with stringers from all the major newspapers. They were everywhere, making it impossible for Emilio to walk about the ship. Slocombe had advised him and Bellucci to keep their mouths shut and not discuss the case with anybody. "Do all your talking in the court." They had, however, prepared a short speech that Emilio would give as a sort of press conference on arrival in Dublin.

The press corps, having temporarily given up the prospect of an interview with Emilio, had switched their attention to the group of Italians who sat in deck chairs on the aft deck. Their spokesmen were two short fat men—the Ziegler brothers, twins, lawyers of some repute hired by Toby Grant to prosecute their case. Grant himself was not on board; he had dispatched George Lloyd to watch over his interests.

At first, the Ziegler brothers revelled in the attention. However, it did not take too long for them to realise that controlling the barrage of questions from the ravenous press men was impossible. The main protagonists—Signors DeMarco, Alonzi, Gambini, Corsini, and Duccio—although well-schooled, in what and what not to say during several long meetings, were a liability. The Zieglers hastily arranged with George Lloyd to take two large cabins, into which they hustled their witnesses. Pursued by the press, the Tweedle Dee and Tweedle Dum lookalike lawyers ushered their charges into the bowels of the steamer, finally managing to squeeze them into the newly hired cabins. Closing the doors and shutting out the press, Anthony Ziegler gave strict instructions.

"Gentlemen, I should not have to explain to you the importance of a unified front. We have gone over the events surrounding the poker game time and time again. You all know what you have to do. It is really quite simple. You all played poker with Scala. He won the last game. Mr DeMarco paid him with a Sweepstake ticket in lieu of cash."

The chubby little lawyer put his hand into the high pockets of his waistcoat and looked into the faces of the witnesses. "Are there any questions? Do you all understand what I have just said?"

DeMarco looked nervous, his moustache twitching slightly. His little feminine hands fluttered at the end of his thick arms. Bernard Ziegler noticed the indecision. "Mr. DeMarco, we have been over this so many times. All you have to do in court is behave as if this man Scala is trying to cheat you out of a huge fortune. Try, if you can, not to look so nervous; be positive. All of you be positive."

Brother Anthony took over. "It is really so simple. Scala won the ticket and agreed to put it in your Sweepstake. You, Mr DeMarco, wrote down his name. You gentlemen saw the whole thing..."

The lesson was interrupted by three deep-throated hoots from the steamer's horn, which announced the arrival of the ship at the harbour of Dun Laoghaire.

Mr. Slocombe of Gaston Sellinger's prestigious firm of London lawyers watched the passengers disembark down the gangplank of the Dublin Castle. An inquisitive crowd of several hundred people had gathered. He waited for the Ziegler brothers to usher their clients from the ship and watched as the press corps took photographs and pleaded for interviews. Satisfied that his client could now leave the ship with a minimum of fuss, he went below to fetch Emilio and Bellucci. The pressmen lay in wait as Mr. Slocombe preceeded Emilio and Bellucci down the gangplank.

"Good evening, gentlemen. Thank you for your patience. Mr. Scala will make a brief statement; I am afraid he will not be answering questions. I am sure you would like to take photographs." Mr. Slocombe stood aside, allowing Emilio to press past him and stand on the bottom step. Flash bulbs popped in a barrage of flashing light, an acrid smoke came from the more old-fashioned photographer's equipment.

Emilio cleared his throat and tried to remember what he had been told not to say by Slocombe. "Gentlemen, gentlemen, please. I'll just make it short. There are some people who say I am a liar and a cheat. I have come here to Ireland with my friend, Signor Bellucci, to prove that I am an honest and very lucky man. God bless you. Thank you."

The photographers crowded around; one pushed forward. "Signor Scala, would you please wave your hat at me?"

The press had got what they wanted, a wonderful picture of the shaven-headed winner of the Irish Sweepstake, smiling and waving to the would-be readers of their various newspapers. The curious crowd loved it, too, cheering on the luckiest man in the world.

Slocombe bustled Emilio and Bellucci through the crowd to a car, where the driver stood holding a sign with the name 'Mr. Slocombe' printed on it. In they climbed, accompanied by the cheers of the crowd. The car nosed its way through the throng, Emilio waving as they called out his name. Bellucci sat back, mesmerised by the reception.

"This is a good sign, Mr. Scala. The people seem to be on your side," said a smiling Mr. Slocombe.

The car drove along the coast towards Blackrock and the city of Dublin. Slocombe spoke clearly with a degree of patience. "I arranged for that court order; the items have been examined as you instructed. The expert will be here tomorrow with his report." Slocombe put the tips of his fingers together and looked out of the car at the unfamiliar sights of the outskirts of Dublin.

"Good. Then we will win," said Emilio as he watched a line of donkey-drawn carts full of turf bring the traffic to a standstill.

"Maybe, Mr Scala, maybe." Slocombe sounded a little uncertain.

Bellucci looked at him, his fat face in need of another shave. "Mr Slocombe, you don't know him. He's a lucky bastard, he will win." The fat man laughed, and Slocombe and Emilio joined him.

## CHAPTER TWENTY FIVE

Scippio carried the last wooden shutter from the yard; slotting it into place, he pushed through the bolt that would hold it to the brick lintel beneath the café window. Satisfied, he pushed an iron bar through the metal rings and snapped a padlock into place. This effectively sealed the café from intruders. He walked back into the yard and knocked on the cottage door. Nazarena came to the door; seeing Scippio, she took a ten-shilling note from her bosom pocket and gave it to him. He handed her the padlock key. "Grazie, Scippio. You are a good boy. Now you take care of yourself."

Scippio took of his cap, looking sad as he thanked Nazarena and walked out of the yard. Selma was dressing the kids in the kitchen as Nazarena closed the door.

"Are you all right with the kids? I nearly finish packing. Then we go."

Selma pulled a woollen jumper over the toddler's head. "Si si. Due minuti. Va bene."

Nazarena climbed the stairs to the bedroom, where she put a few more things in the already half packed battered suitcase. She closed it, struggling with the old bent lock; succeeding, she swung the suitcase off the bed and carried it down the stairs. "Bene. Andiamo. Let's go."

Nazarena put on her hat and coat, then stooped to check and button up the kids' clothes while Selma put her coat on. Nazarena picked up the toddler, then ushered Joe and little Freddy to the door, where she waited for Selma, who followed them out with the suitcase. Joe pulled the yard gates to, and proudly managed the big padlock, carefully closing it through the bolt. He gave his mother the key.

"Va bene. Subito, everybody, or we miss the train."

They crossed the road to the station. Nazarena bought tickets while Joe and Freddy, under Selma's guardianship, looked in and at the huge steam engine waiting at the platform, trickles of steam escaping from the seals at various points of the engine. Nazarena ran along the platform, carrying the baby and ignoring the cries of the newspaper vendor:

"Read all about it! Read all about it! Unlucky Emilio struggles in Sweepstake trial."

Mr. Slocombe had booked Emilio and Bellucci into the Shelbourne Hotel. After making sure that they were checked in, he arranged for a car to pick up his clients in the morning to bring them to the court. He took himself off to his digs over a pub next to the Dublin Four Courts. Emilio and Bellucci tried to have a quiet pint of Guinness in the Shelbourne bar. It proved to be impossible. Within minutes of their arrival, well-wishers surrounded them, the famous Irish hospitality swamping their table with drinks and conversation. Under normal circumstances, Emilio would have really enjoyed this diversion, but he had other things on his mind. He excused himself and, leaving Bellucci to the mercy of a gang of racing aficionados, went up to his room.

Nazarena had not seen him off. Emilio had not been successful in persuading her that he was not having an affair with Willow. He had tried everything he could to pacify her short of cancelling his trip to Dublin, something he could not do. He had been forced to leave her in the cottage; as he closed the door she had screamed that she would be gone when he came back. As he lay down on the hotel bed, he knew she was right. He had been so stupid to try to hide his interest in Willow; he had grossly underestimated his wife's powers of deduction.

The other thing that disturbed him was the way Willow had brushed him off; that had really upset him. He needed to talk to her again. He couldn't leave it like that. She had been so warm and exciting. She had given him a taste of a different world.

Picking up the telephone by the bed, he booked the call, giving the operator Willow's number. She called him back a minute later and put him through. Monique the maid answered the call. He asked for Miss Rutherford. The maid apologised and told him that she had gone away for a few days with Lord St. Ledger.

Emilio put down the telephone and lay back on the bed, wishing that he had a telephone at home so that he could talk to Nazarena. In this condition, he fell asleep.

The next morning Emilio's car pulled up to the steps of the Dublin Four Courts. A huge crowd of well-wishers and the curious had gathered on the pavement. Emilio looked through the car window at the vast crowd, dwarfed by the domed granite building in which his financial fate was to be decided. Slocombe stood on the pavement, surrounded by half a dozen uniformed policemen, and the car nosed its way towards them.

Bellucci looked at the crowd. "They like wearing hats, the Irish."

Emilio smiled as he acknowledged Bellucci's observation. The crowd was a sea of floppy caps and bowlers. The policemen made a semi-circle around the car door, and Emilio gave Bellucci a shove. "You go first; you're bigger than me."

Slocombe opened the door, allowing Bellucci and Emilio to climb out. "Good morning, Mr. Scala, Mr. Bellucci. I have organised a little help, so we should be inside in no time. Stay close together and follow me."

The dapper young clerk led the way; surrounded by the policemen, they carved a path through the noisy but friendly crowd, slowly fighting their way up the steps towards the Four Courts entrance. Photographers crowded around the huge doors, the flashbulbs reflected in bursts from the bevelled glass windows. At last they were inside, though it made no difference; far too many people had been let in. The corridors were packed with all sorts of characters. Slocombe, with the aid of his police escort, hustled Emilio and Bellucci into an anteroom. He thanked the policemen and closed the door.

"We should get a bit of peace in here. We will be starting a half hour late; I applied on your behalf to change the proceedings to court number one. The others were far too small. You seem to have so much support from the crowd, I thought the bigger the audience, the better."

Bellucci had gone to the window, and suddenly began chuckling with laughter. "Come and look at this." He beckoned Emilio over to the window.

From their vantage point through the barred window, they had a perfect view of the Four Courts' steps and the crowd outside. Two cars had pulled up at the pavement. The occupants, without the aid of a police escort, were in all kinds of trouble. Ziegler and Ziegler and the witnesses for the prosecution had made the mistake of getting out of the cars and trying to run the gauntlet of the crowd. Emilio and Bellucci watched in amusement as DeMarco lost his hat. The two chubby lawyers puffed and pushed briefcases held high through the jovial crowd.

Mr. Slocombe decided to get down to business. "Mr. Scala, shall we go through the procedure once more?"

"Si. I think I know what to do; you tell me once more."

In the dressing room of the Judge's private chambers, four elderly Irish men were being transformed into elegant-looking judges with the help of Seamus O'Riordan the court valet. Seamus was almost bald, and what hair he had was plastered onto his skull with brilliantine. His overly tight starched collar had been fastened so well that the flesh and veins of his neck looked to be bursting above the collar's rim. He helped each of the judges in turn. Busily, he adjusted their clothes—the white bands on one, a wig on another. The judges talked among themselves.

"You have yourself a live one today, T. J. All I have is prostitutes, tinkers, and horse thieves."

Another one of the judges, a tall stooped man, joined in. "That's right, T.J. All eyes will be on you. They're calling him the luckiest man in the world."

Seamus held up the black robe for Judge Brendan Meredith. The judge put his arms through the green ribboned sleeves. "He might have been until—" said Seamus, his eyes twinkling, "Until he drew Judge Meredith to hear his case."

The judges laughed as Judge Meredith gave Seamus a good-humoured but stern look over his gold-rimmed half glasses.

"If you look at him like that, Judge, he surely won't tell you a lie." Seamus continued to dress the four old gentlemen, enjoying his privileged position as a court jester to these four powerful men.

The forth judge—who so far had been dressing in silence—took a wee sip from a silver hip flask. "That's me ready, I have a foul murder to contend with, there won't be a laugh in my court today." He adjusted his wig. "Well, T.J., I hope you remember your Latin; they say all of your witnesses only speak Italian."

"Don't worry about me. I will unravel this mystery." He gave his overgrown eyebrows a curl with the thumbs and forefingers of both hands. "Right, Shamus, I'm ready."

Judge Meredith picked up a leather-bound folder of notes.Seamus gave the judge a last brush down as he made his way to the door. "Good day, gentlemen, see you when we adjourn."

The noise of chatter echoed through the corridors as Slocombe led Emilio and Bellucci towards court number one. Emilio's hands were sweating, but apart from this, he felt confident. After all, he was telling the truth. Bellucci patted his friend on the back and grinned as he followed Slocombe and Emilio through the swing doors into the vaulted oak and stone room that was the courtroom. It was packed to capacity; every available seat was taken. Emilio looked up at the gallery, where a mass of chattering faces looked down at him.

Slocombe led the way to an oak table opposite the bench, and they took their seats. Emilio looked over to the opposition. Ziegler and Ziegler sat at a similar oak table, DeMarco with them. Directly behind the Ziegler brothers sat Duccio, Corsini, Alonzi, and Gambini. George Lloyd sat behind them.

Emilio rubbed the moisture from his hands on his trousers as the court usher entered with Judge Meredith from a door behind the bench. The chatter in the court seemed to reach a crescendo, punctuated with echoing coughs. Judge Meredith banged his gavel on the bench, the crack of it bouncing off the stone walls, and the noise dropped like a blanket. What remained was low chattering rumble; into this, the usher announced that the court was in session. The rumbling chatter in the church of a courtroom slid down the audio scale until Emilio could hear the clock tick.

Emilio had been able to sit and watch the early part of the proceedings, absorbing the atmosphere of the court. Mr. Slocombe occasionally leaned over and whispered an explanation or defined a point of law.

Judge Meredith looked fearsome behind his half spectacles. His bushy eyebrows twitched as he asked the question. "Let me get this clear. If I sold a book containing ten Sweepstake tickets, the Sweep organisers would give me, for my trouble, one free ticket, for myself. A ticket that would have exactly the same chance and entitlement of winning a prize as all the other tickets purchased by members of the public for good money."

The Ziegler brothers listened intently to the judge. They had a curious way of working, appearing to speak in turns, never interrupting each other or getting in each other's way. Bernard Ziegler answered the Judge. "That is correct, Your Honour."

The Judge put his fingers together in thought. "'Tis no wonder so many tickets were sold. Please proceed, Messrs Ziegler."

Anthony Ziegler took the floor. "The prize that is in dispute, amounts to three hundred and fifty-five thousand, four hundred and ten pounds. Plus two thousand pounds that Emilio Scala has already received, his prize for drawing a horse in the Sweepstake. Each of my ten clients is claiming one-eleventh part of that total amount. Thirty-two thousand four hundred and ninety pounds, your honour."

The judge, eyes twinkling, continued to spell things out. "May I inquire as to who holds the eleventh part?"

Bernard Ziegler answered. "Mr. Scala, Your Honour.."

Judge Meredith looked over his highly polished lenses at Emilio. "So. Mr. Scala, if this court were to decide against you, you would still receive a sum equal to that of any of the plaintiffs?"

Slocombe whispered in Emilio's ear. Emilio stood up "No, Your Honour. I have lost half of it to a bookmaker."

A titter of amusement at Emilio's apparent misfortune rippled through the court. Judge Meredith stopped it from spreading by banging his gavel on the bench. "That is unfortunate, but irrelevant. Messrs Ziegler, would you please call your next witness."

Emilio sat down as the court usher called Adamo DeMarco to the stand. He watched impassively as DeMarco took his oath in Italian, answering preliminary questions truthfully in broken English, until Bernard Ziegler homed in on his witness.

"Mr. DeMarco, would you tell the court how you came about idea to make your own sweepstake?"

DeMarco addressed the court in his sandpaper voice. "Yes, sir. I think it would be a good idea to sell some sweep tickets to some friends and to keep all the tickets in a syndicate, so that if one wins we all win. Firstly, I make up this card which say 'DeMarco's Sweepstake Lottery' and I hang it up in my shop. Then Franco come in for a shave, I tell him my idea and he say give me one. So I put him, he give me ten shillings, and I write his name and number down. Then I do the same with Corsini, and Alonzi, then Gambini, and so, and so. Then slowly slowly I sell all the tickets, except one, that is my free ticket."

"Mr DeMarco," continued Anthony Ziegler, "would you tell the court what happened to that last ticket?"

DeMarco's little fingers danced nervously on the rail in front of him. "Yes, sir. About the second week in January, I was playing poker with the boys in the shop. Scala comes in and sit down and we deal him in, we play all day going up and down, you know. Then Scala, he win a big pot. When I fold two pairs, he win and send me skint. So I pay him a pound short by accident. Then I show him my ticket and say, here, you take this. Then I tell him about my lottery and he say put me in. So I write his name down and put his number on the list."

Bernard Ziegler walked to the witness. "You put Mr. Scala's name and number on the list. What happened next?"

"Nothing happened next. We just wait two months with the list hanging on the wall. We wait for the sweepstake draw, which happen on the thirteenth of March. The next day I see in the newspaper that the Scala ticket has drawn the horse Grakle. So I go round to see Scala to tell him that we win two thousand pounds. He say he knows, and that a man from the sweep has been to see him, and that he got the money. I ask him when he want to do the share out. He tell me to fuck off."

For the usual reason, the crowded court laughed at the last remark, but were soon halted by a loud crack of Judge Meredith's gavel. "Thank you, Mr DeMarco, please continue."

"Anyway, he say I should forget about it 'cause I got no proof. I say he's a liar, and I say I got witnesses. He say screw the witnesses, you need proof in writing. I tell him he's a crook, and here I am."

Anthony Ziegler approached the witness. "Mr. Scala made it quite clear that he had no intention of paying you.

Judge Meredith leaned forward on his bench. "Mr. Ziegler. What Mr.

Scala made clear was that he disagreed with Mr. DeMarco. The witness may proceed."

DeMarco's face had begun to bead up; he removed some of the moisture with the back of his hand. "Yes, sir. I tell him he is a liar. We have a row and I leave empty-handed back to my shop to tell Gambini and Alonzi that Scala is trying to screw us."

Emilio and Bellucci watched the performance, looking at each other and acknowledging their anger.

Barnard Ziegler took over. "Thank you, Mr. DeMarco. Just one more thing; I would like to call for exhibit A."

The usher went to the side of the court and fetched the sweep card. He undid the brown paper wrapping and handed it to DeMarco. "Have you seen that before?" asked Bernard Ziegler.

"Yes, sir. That is my lottery card. It has all the names and numbers written on it."

Judge Meredith was curios. "May I have a look at the exhibit?"

Anthony Ziegler took the card to the Judge, who studied it closely.

The next witness called was Alfredo Alonzi, whose English was very bad. He entertained the court with his animated broken English.

"How long have you known Mr. DeMarco?" asked Anthony Ziegler.

"When I come to England in twenty-six." Alonso's ears wagged as he spoke.

"That would be about five years. Now then, how long have you known Mr. Scala?"

Alonso's ears moved in time to his jaw. "The same time. I work for

Scala when I first come. I sell ice cream for him."

Bernard Ziegler indicated the other witnesses. "How well do you know these gentlemen?"

"I see them every week since I come here. We play cards and we live in the same, er.. street."

Anthony Ziegler smiled reassuringly at Alonso's peanut face. "Now, I want you to tell me how you came to buy your sweepstake ticket and who you bought it from?"

"DeMarco, he sell me the ticket for ten shillings, and he say he gonna put my ticket in the pot with the other customers. He say if one wins we all win."

Bernard Ziegler strolled around the floor to get a bit more attention. "Did you get a receipt for your ticket from Mr. DeMarco? Or did you make any kind of agreement other than a verbal one?"

Alonzi looked confused, searching the faces of the other witnesses for help. "What is.... agreement?"

Corsini stood up and shouted an explanation of the question in Italian. Alonzi understood. "No. No contrato. It's DeMarco, I trust him. If he say he put me on his list, he put me on his list."

Anthony Ziegler came to him. "Were you present when Scala got his ticket?"

"He won it in the poker game, with a pair of twos. He say to DeMarco, 'Put it in the pot.' We all see him."

"Was there a contract?"

"No. No contrato. He trust DeMarco like all the boys."

Judge Meredith heard all the prosecution witnesses tell the same story. His ulcer was playing up, and he needed food and milk. He listened to Corsini explain that Emilio Scala had been a good friend until he drew the sweepstake horse; then he became greedy and claimed all the money for himself. Judge Meredith had heard enough from the prosecution. He called an adjournment for lunch, telling the defence that they could put their case at two o'clock.

Slocombe had arranged for coffee and sandwiches to be brought to the private room, and they were waiting on the only table: thick-cut slices of soda bread, a plate covered in slices of ham and a hunk of cheese. Bellucci went for the coffee jug, changed his mind, and grabbed one of the three bottles of Guinness. With his free hand, he built a sandwich and was suddenly happy. Emilio wasn't hungry; he poured himself a coffee and sat in silence until Slocombe returned.

"The good news is that your witness definitely caught the boat. He should be here any minute; if he is late, you will just have to keep calling witnesses. Now, shall we go over what you are going to do?"

Emilio drained his coffee and nodded at Slocombe. Bellucci noticed Emilio's apprehension. With a mouth full of sandwich, he goaded his friend into action.

"Paesane! Play your part. You always want to be an actor. Now you have a chance. Those liars, you piss on them, you see. Eat something. I make you a sandwich; this ham is very good."

Emilio declined and moved with Slocombe to the bench under the window.

If anything, the court was more crushed than it had been for the morning session. The plaintiffs and the defendant were already seated when Judge Meredith entered through the door in the panelling at the back of the court. The usher stepped forward. "Ladies and gentlemen, this court is now in session. Judge Brendan Meredith is presiding."

The Judge pushed his spectacles on to the bridge of his nose. "This morning, the court heard the case put forward by the plaintiffs. Mr. Scala, would you care to proceed for the defendant?"

Emilio gave Slocombe a nervous look and then stood up and walked to the bench. "Thank you, Your Honour. I have not done anything like this before, please excuse me if I am nervous."

This brought a titter of laughter from the crowded court. Emilio continued. "I would like to call myself as my first witness. Signor Emilio Scala."

Emilio looked at the laughing sea of faces in front of him, not sure whether they were laughing with him or at him. He continued, and carefully told his story, He described his day at the Grand National and how he had nearly sold part of his ticket, and how he kept it and watched Grakle win the race; he described the joy and the euphoria he felt as it sank in that he had won the biggest prize in history. He went on to tell the court of the moment in Mr. Carter's office when he went to collect his cheque and was told of the claim by DeMarco and the boys. He described his shock and anger and disappointment and how he had then become resolved to come to Ireland to defend his name and his prize.

Judge Meredith listened patiently. The two pints of milk he had drunk at lunch had stopped his ulcer speaking to him. Finally the Judge asked The Ziegler brothers if they would care to cross-examine the witness.

Anthony Ziegler took the floor. "Mr. Scala, will you look at exhibit

A." Anthony Ziegler passed Emilio the sweepstake card. Emilio took it and looked at it. "Is your name on it?"

Emilio saw his name. "Yes, but—"

Bernard Ziegler interrupted him. "Would you please just answer my questions? Why did you wait until you drew a horse in the sweepstake before you objected to it being there?"

Emilio's face had grown angry. "I didn't object. I didn't know. I go to DeMarco's only once before the draw for a haircut."

The packed room burst into laughter. Emilio realised why they had laughed. He ran his hand self-consciously over his shaved head. "But I never look closely at the card. I made some remark about how terrific it would be to win the sweep. Then while he cut my hair, he tells me how much he gets if one of the boys wins. I tell him if I win, I get three hundred and fifty thousand pounds."

Bernard Ziegler flippantly asked the next question. "Can anyone corroborate your story?"

Emilio didn't understand corroborate. "Eh?" he said.

"Have you any witnesses to back up your story?"

"No."

The Ziegler brothers played to the gallery, both of them pompously glancing around the court. "None," said Bernard

"So all the witnesses are lying?" said Anthony.

"That doesn't mean it's not true. They want to cheat me out of my prize."

"So everyone but you is lying. Ten people are all lying."

Emilio looked at the court. "Yes."

"Thank you." Both Zieglers retired smugly to their seats.

Emilio looked tired and frustrated; he looked at Slocombe, who in turn looked around the court. He shook his head negatively at Emilio.

Emilio looked over to Judge Meredith. "Now I would like to ask DeMarco a few things."

The Judge put him right. "You mean that you would like to call the next witness."

To a background of laughter, Emilio said, "Yes, please. Mr. DeMarco. I'm sorry, am I doing okay?"

Judge Meredith allowed himself a smile. "You will find that out in due course." The judge brought down his gavel. "Can I have quiet in the court?"

The usher called DeMarco to the stand. Emilio went over to Slocombe and had a whispered word, while DeMarco went in to the box.

"I don't know," said Slocombe. "He should be here any minute, just take as long as you can with DeMarco."

Slocombe tried to smile in the hope of reassuring Emilio, but it didn't work. Emilio turned back to DeMarco, looking worried. He went to the exhibit table and picked up exhibit A, taking it over to DeMarco. "Mr. DeMarco you have seen this card before, yes? Is this your handwriting?"

DeMarco didn't bother to look at the card. "Yes, I make this card."

"I know you did. I agree with you. But you put my name on it after you heard that I draw Grakle in the sweepstake."

DeMarco did a good job of being outraged. "You are lying. You are trying to swindle us."

Emilio walked away towards the Judge. "Your Honour, I would like to show exhibit B." Emilio was getting into this; he had watched the Zieglers all morning and was doing a fair imitation of a swaggering lawyer.

Emilio caught a signal from Slocombe as the usher walked to the exhibit table. Slocombe wagged his thumb, indicating the room behind him. Emilio followed the thumb's direction and then smiled. He turned to DeMarco and approached him, taking the exhibit from the usher on the way. "Mr. DeMarco, have you seen this before?"

Emilio held out the exhibit; it was the watch from the barbershop.

"Yes, it is my watch, from my shop."

Emilio shook it and listened. "Does it work?"

DeMarco pulled a face, wondering what this had to do with anything. "Sometimes," he croaked.

"You mean, it doesn't work?

"Sometimes it works," answered the agitated barber. "It just keeps stopping, and I wind it up, then it go, then it stop, so I get fed up and hang it on the wall. So what?"

Emilio did a Ziegler and turned away from the witness. "Thank you, Mr. DeMarco. You can sit down." Emilio turned to Judge Meredith. "Your Honour, can I have one more witness?"

Judge Meredith, so relieved to be free from the ulcer pain was smiling. "You may call as many as you like so long as you think they will help you." The judge lowered his glasses and looked at the usher. "You may call the next witness."

Slocombe stood up and handed the usher a piece of paper. The usher took it and read from it. "I call Professor George Gough to the stand."

A tall thin man with slightly stooped shoulders came from the back of the court. A nest of pens poked from the top pocket of his dark grey suit. He was clean-shaven with strip of hair that used to be a widow's peak stretching back across his otherwise bald head. The knobs of his cheekbones stuck out from his thin face, serving as a rest for the shafts of his horn-rimmed spectacles. Emilio watched him walk to the witness box where he took his oath which he appeared to know by heart.

Emilio approached the witness; now he actually looked like a lawyer, he was confident and held himself differently. "Professor," he said enjoying the use of the word. "Can you tell the court, please, what is your job?"

The Professor's head wobbled and then rested back on his neck like a stork's. "I am a forensic scientist. And have been with Scotland Yard for twenty-five years; for ten of those, I have headed their forensic department."

Emilio moved towards him. "Excuse me, professor, please explain what is forensic."

"In my case, it means the scientific study of evidence of crimes."

"Then it is your job to examine little details in crimes and things like that? For the Scotland Yard."

The Professor's head wobbled and came to rest. "Yes, it was and still is. I am now a consultant on a freelance basis to police forces all over the world."

Emilio looked triumphant; this was a serious man. "Professor, would you mind looking at exhibit B?"

The usher brought the exhibit to the stand and gave it to the Professor. The professor examined it. "Yes, I have examined this watch. I found that its working movement had been impaired by a fine dust, which consisted of approximately fifty percent human hair. This dust was so fine that it had penetrated the machined joints at both the back and the front of the watch."

"What does that mean, Professor?"

"Only that the watch had been kept in an environment that contained a lot of human hair dust in its atmosphere."

"A barber shop?" Emilio looked at the professor

"Yes, a barber shop, a wig factory, a ladies' hairdresser."

"So in these places, there is always this human hair dust floating about."

"Yes. The amount would depend largely on the amount of haircutting activity in relation to the size and ventilation of the premises."

"But in this place, the place where this watch lived, there was enough to eventually stop it.

"Yes, in this case that is correct."

Emilio, now very confident looked across to DeMarco as he thanked the professor. "Can I now ask you to look at exhibit A? The list. What can you tell us about this?" Emilio handed him the card.

Professor Gough studied it for a moment, rearranged his glasses, and put the list down. "Yes, I have studied this and the writing thereon, both chemically and microscopically, in order to ascertain if any alterations had been made to it. My chemical tests proved negative. All the names and numbers had been written by the same hand, pen, and ink."

Emilio, with a straight face, looked over to DeMarco, who looked pleased, as did the Zieglers. The Professor wobbled his head and continued. "The microscopic tests, however, revealed that the last entry on the list, namely the name EMILIO SCALA, and the number V.T.32159, had been added some time after the other ten names.

Emilio's next question was drowned by an excited murmur from the court. Judge Meredith gave his gavel a crack on the bench. "Can I have this court quiet? Mr. Scala, you were saying."

"Can you say how long after?"

"No, but what I can say is that the very same hair dust that stopped the watch has, over a period of time, adhered to the board that the list is written on, covering the surface with a layer of dust, quite visible under an ordinary microscope. At least, it has to the first ten names. It is quite clear that the last entry was made on top of that layer of dust; on further examination, I found that the amount of dust on top of the last addition was quite negligible."

Judge Meredith used his gavel to stop the mounting chatter. "I will have order in this court; if I don't get it I will clear it. Now then. Mr Scala."

"I have nothing more to say to the witness except to thank him and the court for giving me this opportunity to defend my name against these people, these very unlucky people who nearly won the sweepstake. And because they nearly won it, they got eaten by envy and tempted into lying and cheating to try to take my prize away."

The court went into the sort of uproar that happens in public places; even Judge Meredith's gavel lost its voice. Slocombe jumped to his feet as the judge ordered the court servants to restore order. "If you please, Your Honour, Mr Scala would like to press for a motion that this case be dismissed and that you find in favour of the defendant."

The mayhem abated as the servants went about their business. Judge Meredith felt the first pangs of his ulcer coming on; he was not going to prolong these proceedings. His mind was made up, as he gave vent to the gavel. "Silence in court!" he bellowed, causing an acid burn in his chest, but it silenced the courtroom.

"Professor Gough, you may step down." The Judge looked at the row of Italians and their two chubby Old Bailey lawyers, lowering his head to look over his gold spectacles. He then turned his eyes on the beaming Emilio. "I have listened to a story that would do credit to the best of fiction, a story of friends who fall out over one of their number's good fortune. I have listened to passionate pleas of liar, cheat. I have listened. Thankfully, the scrupulous evidence of Professor Gough has, in my mind, made it quite clear that the defendant is the luckiest man in the world and is quite entitled to keep his prize. I find in favour of the defendant."

The judge closed his book with a snap. "This court is dismissed."

Judge Meredith swept out through the panelled door, leaving the courtroom in chaos; Bellucci lifted Emilio up like a doll and spun him into Slocombe, who would have preferred a more dignified end to a successful defence. He attempted to push Bellucci, still carrying Emilio, out of the court.

Emilio wriggled free and turned towards DeMarco and the Zieglers. "Hey, Paesanes. No hard feelings. You win some, you lose some, what do you say?" Emilio's greeting drew no positive reaction, though he didn't really expect any. DeMarco and Corsini looked away. "Please yourselves. If you need anything you come and see me."

Emilio put on his hat and followed Slocombe and Bellucci out of the court and into the flagstoned corridor. High in the ceiling, circular skylights filtered sunshine onto the heads of the crowd; the light spilled onto the panelled walls and made rainbow spectrums in the bevelled edges of the thick glass windows that were set in some of the doors. The spectrums were greatest in the main doors at the end of the long corridor, and the brightness threw the profiles of the crowd into silhouette. Slocombe and Bellucci pushed a way through the crowd, making room for Emilio.

"Congratulations, Emilio." The voice cut through the din, not by its volume but by its bright female clarity.

Emilio turned his head, There she was, looking marvellous as usual. "We had to come, in case you needed us. We were worried about you."

Lord St.Ledger stepped forward his hand held out. "It's congratulations for you and congratulations for me. Willow has promised to marry me; we are officially engaged."

Emilio took St. Ledger's hand and shook it. "You are right, we have both had a very good day; may I kiss your future bride?"

St. Ledger smiled as Emilio kissed Willow on the cheek, putting his outstretched arms behind Emilio and Willow as if to propel them along the now less crowded corridor. "Come, let's go somewhere to celebrate."

"Congratulations, Mr. Scala." It was Toby Grant; he stepped into the light. "Your Lordship, Miss Rutherford."

Emilio looked at him. "Ah. The bookmaker, I have been expecting you." Emilio gave Grant a penetrating look.

"Good, then you have something for me?" Grant produced the I.O.U.

"Yes, Mr Grant." Emilio reached into a pocket and produced his chequebook; he borrowed Bellucci's shoulder and wrote the cheque. Tearing it from the book, he waved it at Grant.

"Fifteen thousand, wasn't it?" Grant smiled the smile of a shark.

"I've made this out for thirty thousand."

Grant looked a little surprised, as did Willow, St. Ledger, and Bellucci. Emilio took a half-crown coin from his pocket and fingered it. He looked into Grant's greedy face. "Are you a gambler or just a bookmaker?" Emilio fingered the silver coin. "We spin double or nothing. Unless that's too rich for you?"

Grant was trapped; he had been hit with his own phraseology in front of St.Ledger and Willow, and hesitated momentarily. "Suits me. I'll spin, you call." Grant took the coin and spun it in the air; catching it, he slapped it down on the back of his hand. There was a brief silence as all eyes focused on the bookmakers' knuckles.

"Heads." Emilio said in a calm cool voice.

The bookmaker lifted his manicured hand from the coin. The shining head of Queen Victoria twinkled in the light from the overhead window.

Emilio tore up the cheque and the I.O.U. "Thank you, Mr. Grant." Emilio turned to his friends. "Shall we go and celebrate?" He led the way along the corridor towards the main doors. Bellucci ran after him with a grin on his face like a cheese.

There were people outside on the steps; Emilio could see the misshapen, refracting shapes bobbing and moving in the bevelled windows of the doors. The shapes became clearer with each stride; he was moving fast now, spurred on by a kind of premonition. Reaching the doors, he flung them open.

Nazarena and Selma stood on the steps at the front of the crowd. Little Joe saw his father first and ran the few yards to him like a whippet, flinging his little arms around Emilio's legs; Freddy followed with Nazarene. Selma carried the baby. Nazarene rushed into Emilio's outstretched arms; he hugged her and lifted her from the ground, tears of joy running down his face as he felt the strength of his boys hugging his legs.

He put his wife down and turned to his friends. "I would like to introduce you to my wife."

Nazarene looked suspiciously at the beautiful Willow and the tall distinguished-looking man at her side. "Lord St. Ledger and his fiancé, Wilhelmina Rutherford; my wife, Nazarena Scala."

Nazarena nervously shook their hands. 'Fiancé, it was true; she is another man's woman,' Nazarena thought as she let go of Willow's smooth hand.

Emilio turned to Bellucci. "Don't leave Selma standing there, she come a long way to see you. Go on, propose to her, I give you the finest wedding money can buy."

Bellucci approached Selma her cheeks glowing under her dark soulful eyes; the fat man looked back for support.

"Go on, idioto, she has been waiting for years."

Bellucci put his fat arm around her shoulder and kissed her rosy cheek.

"Come on, everybody, we go celebrate."

Flashbulbs popped as reporters fired questions to the happy party following Slocombe down the steps to the waiting cars.

Emilio Scala and his family were driven away into their new life.

# ABOUT THE AUTHOR

Mim Scala: born in Fulham London 1940, of Italian parents, Started life in The Cosmopolitan North End Road Market where his Parents ran the famous SCALA'S ice cream parlour. Studied briefly at Chelsea School of Art and then in his late teens left the confines of home to find his way in the exciting London of the late 50's, He was one of the first hosts of private gaming parties in fashionable Chelsea, mixing easily with Chelsea society and Soho gangsters. Confronted by the Kray Twins Mim traveled to Spain and then Morocco before returning to london to become part of the burgeoning sixties.Mim Became a Theatrical agent and acquired the film rights to the Peter O'Donnell cartoon strip Modesty Blaise, The Film had an inspirational influence on the young Quentin Tarantino. Who has used the Blaise influences in all his films including Pulp Fiction. Mim then Founded The Scala Brown Associates Theatrical Agency in 1966. 1977 Mim Together with Cupid Films packaged the Jean Luc Godard Film Sympathy for the devil with the Rolling Stones. The end of the sixties saw mim take off from his agency desk to travel the world . Returning to England in 1973 Mim Founded ESP music an agency dedicated to the management of record producers, his clients included Chris Kimsey (Rolling Stones.) Stewart Levine (Simply Red BB King etc.) Jimmi Miller (Rolling Stones Beggars Banquet etc) Mim now lives in Ireland with his wife Janie , and his son Fred and their horses and dogs.

www.mimscala.co.uk

Other works by Mim Scala

Diary of a Teddy Boy 2000 https://www.createspace.com/3946601

Bibi a sixties novel : 2012 : https://www.createspace.com/3939102

For reviews go to www.mimscala.co.uk

Made in the USA
San Bernardino, CA
25 March 2013